"You Don't Hav[e] Me, Faith. You'[...] I'll Stay In Here While You Change."

The sound of Cooper's deep baritone saying her name sent a shiver up Faith's spine and had her scurrying into the living room to find dry clothes. Cooper might not think of himself as the threatening type, but she knew better. Physically, she had no doubt, he would keep his promise. How she knew that, she wasn't sure. She just did.

But the fact that he practically oozed virility from every pore of his skin had her concerned. She didn't want to find Cooper Adams attractive, didn't want to think of him as honorable or trustworthy. In fact, she didn't want to think of him at all. Her peace of mind depended on it.

But the memory of his body pressed to hers, the smell of his clean masculine skin and the integrity she'd detected in his deep blue eyes wouldn't allow her to forget....

Dear Reader,

Dog days of summer got you down? Chill out and relax with six brand-new love stories from Silhouette Desire!

August's MAN OF THE MONTH is the first book in the exciting family-based saga BECKETT'S FORTUNE by Dixie Browning. *Beckett's Cinderella* features a hero honor-bound to repay a generations-old debt and a poor-but-proud heroine leery of love and money she can't believe is offered unconditionally. *His E-Mail Order Wife* by Kristi Gold, in which matchmaking relatives use the Internet to find a high-powered exec a bride, is the latest title in the powerful DYNASTIES: THE CONNELLYS series.

A daughter seeking revenge discovers love instead in *Falling for the Enemy* by Shawna Delacorte. Then, in *Millionaire Cop & Mom-To-Be* by Charlotte Hughes, a jilted, pregnant bride is rescued by her childhood sweetheart.

Passion flares between a family-minded rancher and a marriage-shy divorcée in Kathie DeNosky's *Cowboy Boss*. And a pretend marriage leads to undeniable passion in *Desperado Dad* by Linda Conrad.

So find some shade, grab a cold one…and read all six passionate, powerful and provocative new love stories from Silhouette Desire this month.

Enjoy!

Joan Marlow Golan

Joan Marlow Golan
Senior Editor, Silhouette Desire

Please address questions and book requests to:
Silhouette Reader Service
U.S.: 3010 Walden Ave., P.O. Box 1325, Buffalo, NY 14269
Canadian: P.O. Box 609, Fort Erie, Ont. L2A 5X3

Cowboy Boss
KATHIE DeNOSKY

Silhouette® Desire®

Published by Silhouette Books

America's Publisher of Contemporary Romance

SILHOUETTE BOOKS

ISBN 0-373-76457-X

COWBOY BOSS

Copyright © 2002 by Kathie DeNosky

Books by Kathie DeNosky

Silhouette Desire

Did You Say Married?! #1296
The Rough and Ready Rancher #1355
His Baby Surprise #1374
Maternally Yours #1418
Cassie's Cowboy Daddy #1439
Cowboy Boss #1457

KATHIE DeNOSKY

lives in deep southern Illinois with her husband and three children. After reading and enjoying Silhouette books for many years, she is ecstatic about being able to share her stories with others as a Silhouette Desire author. Highly sensual stories with a generous amount of humor, Kathie's books have appeared on the Waldenbooks bestseller list. She enjoys going to rodeos, traveling to research settings for her books and listening to country music. She often starts her day at 2:00 a.m., so she can write without interruption, before the rest of the family is up and about. You may write to Kathie at P.O. Box 2064, Herrin, Illinois 62948-5264 or e-mail her at kathie@kathiedenosky.com.

To Carolyn Columbo-Baziluk, Jack Van,
Mona Smith and Harrison Norris.
Thank you for teaching me the beauty of reading books
and the skills needed to write them.

And a special thank-you to Helen Galloway
for inspiring me to reach for the stars.

One

Cooper Adams had stared death square in the face and lived to tell about it. But his recovery from a run-in with the meanest, nastiest rodeo bull the good Lord ever blessed with the breath of life, couldn't compare with the uphill battle he faced now.

He turned to glare at the old man standing next to him. "Whiskers, what on God's green earth ever possessed you to buy this dump? And with *my* money."

"Now, Coop, don't go gettin' your nose outta joint." Obviously unperturbed by Cooper's disgusted tone, Whiskers Penn flashed a toothless grin. "Like I told you on the phone, the Triple Bar might not look like much right now, but it's got a lotta maybe in it."

Cooper snorted. "Yeah, *maybe* the house and

barns won't fall down with the first stiff wind that comes along.''

He stared at the house that had been purchased with his hard-earned money. To say the place had seen better days was an understatement.

Huge strips of peeling paint flapped in the breeze. The windows—what few that weren't broken—were so coated with dry Texas dust they were opaque. And the back porch roof sagged ominously on one end from a broken support post. But that wasn't the worst of it. There were so many shingles missing, Cooper had no doubt the place leaked like a sieve when it rained.

He pushed his tan Resistol back off his forehead and planted his hands on his hips as he mentally calculated how much money it would take to make it livable. By the time he hit the five figure mark, he cringed. There went the second truck he'd planned to buy before winter.

Damn! He'd counted on being moved in by the time his brother-in-law, Flint McCray, got back from taking Cooper's sister Jenna and their boys to Disneyworld. That was only a week away and Cooper still had the pastures to fence before Flint brought the cattle over from the Rocking M.

"Well, I'm gonna mosey on up to Amarillo," Whiskers said, checking his watch. "I oughtta have just enough time to pick up them fencin' supplies you wanted."

Cooper nodded. "While you're at it, pick up a couple of rolls of heavy plastic."

The old man chuckled. "You thinkin' on coverin' some of them places where the shingles are missin', are ya?"

"And the windows," Cooper said, nodding. "The weather report said it's supposed to start raining and continue through the week. I don't want the interior damaged any more than it already is before I can get around to making repairs."

"I coulda told you it was gonna rain without havin' to listen to a danged old weather report," Whiskers said, limping toward Cooper's pickup. "My joints are painin' me somethin' fierce and it's put a real bad hitch in my get-along."

Cooper watched the bowlegged old cowboy slowly climb into the truck and start the engine. Pulling the truck to a stop beside Cooper, Whiskers grinned. "Looks like you're about to get some company."

Turning, Cooper watched a red truck bounce down the narrow road leading to his new home—such as it was. The truck bottomed out in a pothole deep enough to bury a full-grown mule before coming to a stop beside some fence posts holding up some broken boards—the corral. Something else he'd have to fix.

"Probably the authorities coming to condemn this place," he said, glancing at the old man.

Whiskers gave Cooper an ear-to-ear toothless grin that made the hair on the back of Cooper's neck tingle. "Don't shame me, boy. Just be sure you mind your manners, ya hear?"

"Howdy!" A burly looking man of about fifty got out of the red truck and started removing luggage from the back. "Name's Bubba West. I'm your neighbor to the east."

"What the hell's going on here?" Cooper demanded.

"Looks to me like somebody's fixin' to stay a spell," Whiskers said, sounding a little too innocent. He cackled as if he found something highly amusing, gunned the engine, then pulled around the red truck before Cooper could stop him.

When the dust settled, Cooper frowned. Had Whiskers finally gone around the bend?

He dismissed that idea immediately. He'd known the old geezer for over five years and, if anything, Whiskers's mind got sharper with age. No, he definitely had something up his sleeve and wanted to make a fast getaway. Cooper just didn't know what that something was, or what it had to do with him. He did, however, know that as sure as the sun rose in the east, he wasn't going to like it when he found out.

Cooper opened his mouth to stop Bubba, but the sight of a young woman exiting the passenger side struck him speechless. He'd been so preoccupied with what Whiskers was up to, Cooper hadn't noticed there was a second person in the truck. But he sure as hell noticed now. When she turned to say something to Bubba, her long, wavy auburn hair brushed the middle of her back and drew Cooper's attention to the best-looking backside he'd seen in years. Maybe ever.

Tall and slender, she wasn't skinny like those pencil-thin models he'd seen in magazines and on television. No, this was a woman with enough curves to drive a man to the brink of insanity. Her hips flared just enough to draw attention to the narrowness of her waist, tight little rear and long blue-jeans clad legs. Shapely as hell legs. The wrap-around-a-man-and-take-him-to-heaven kind of legs.

Cooper gulped hard and shook his head to clear it. He couldn't hear what she'd said to Bubba, but it was clear the suitcases were hers. Cooper started to protest, but she moved to face him and he couldn't have formed words if his life depended on it. She wasn't just attractive. The woman was downright gorgeous.

Her full mouth and sensuous lips curving in a slight smile, made his mouth go dry. But it was her eyes that damn near knocked his size thirteen boots right off his feet. Big, brown eyes stared at him expectantly and made him want to do something stupid like slay a dragon or move a mountain for her.

"See ya 'round, neighbor," Bubba said with a wave. When had the man stopped pulling bags from the truck and climbed back into the cab?

Brought back to his senses by the growl of the powerful engine turning over, Cooper tried to stop him. "Hey—"

But it was too late. Bubba was already turning the truck around and heading back down the lane, leaving a cloud of Panhandle dust swirling in his wake.

Cooper and the woman stared at each other for several long seconds before he finally managed to make his feet move toward her. "I'm Cooper—"

"I'm Faith—"

They both stopped to stare at each other.

Laughing, Cooper extended his hand. "Let's try this again. I'm Cooper Adams."

She smiled and placed her hand in his. "And I'm Faith Broderick."

As soon as her soft skin came into contact with his callused palm, heat streaked up his arm, then headed straight to the region south of his belt buckle.

He quickly released her hand. To his satisfaction, she had trouble meeting his eyes and seemed to take a great interest in the strap of her shoulder bag. He took it as a sign she'd been as shaken by the contact as he'd been.

Feeling a little better just knowing he wasn't the only one affected, he asked, "What can I do for you, Ms. Broderick?"

She glanced toward the lane leading to the main road. "Was that Mr. Penn I saw leaving in the black truck?"

Her voice was so soft and sexy that Cooper found himself having to swallow several times before he could force words past the cotton coating his mouth and throat. Nodding, he said, "Whiskers went up to Amarillo for fencing supplies."

"Oh." She suddenly looked uncertain. "Did he say when he'd return?"

Cooper smiled in an effort to reassure her. "He should be back before dark. Is there something I could help you with?"

"I don't think so." She shook her head and gave him a smile that damned near knocked the breath out of him. She nervously fingered the strap on her shoulder bag. "I really should talk to Mr. Penn. Did he give you any instructions before he left?"

Cooper laughed. "He's never been at a loss for telling me what to do or how to do it. And out of respect for his age, I listen, then do what *I* think is best."

Her smile faded. "He lets you get away with that?" she asked, clearly incredulous.

"Oh, he can get kind of mouthy about it sometimes." Cooper shrugged. "I just let him spout off and ignore most of it."

"I've never had a boss that lenient," she said, shaking her head. "It's going to take some getting used to."

He suddenly felt like they were carrying on two completely different conversations. "You think I work for Whiskers?"

"Don't you?"

Cooper frowned. "No. When he's not trying to run my life, he works for my brother-in-law, Flint McCray."

She shook her head as if she didn't believe him. "When he hired me, Mr. Penn said he needed someone to keep his house and do the cooking for the Triple Bar Ranch."

"He did what?!" Cooper felt like the ground had dropped from beneath his boots. He glanced at the suitcases. He'd forgotten all about them once she'd treated him to her sexy smile.

She placed her hand to her chest and started backing away from him. Well, hell. The last thing he'd meant to do was scare her.

"Look, Ms. Broderick, I'm sorry if I frightened you. I certainly didn't mean to. But I'm the owner of the Triple Bar Ranch." He glanced over his shoulder at the house. "And as you can see, I won't be needing a housekeeper for quite some time."

The ringing of his cell phone stopped Cooper from saying anything further. Releasing the clip on the side of his belt, he snapped it open and punched the talk button.

Before he had the chance to say a word, Whiskers's voice crackled across the line and into his ear.

"Coop, I'm bettin' your purty sore at me and Bubba 'bout now."

Cooper glanced at Faith. She looked like a skittish colt—ready to bolt at the slightest provocation. And if she didn't stop fiddling with the strap on her shoulder bag, she'd twist the damned thing clean in two.

Instead of the tongue-lashing he wanted to give Whiskers, Cooper said tightly, "You could say that."

Whiskers chuckled. "I figured you would be. That's why I'm gonna mosey on back to the Rocking M and wait for Flint and Jenna to get back from vacation. It'll give you time to cool off and get to know that little gal. I'll come back down to the Triple Bar when Flint brings the cattle next week."

Cooper glanced at Faith and tried to give her a reassuring smile, but he was pretty sure it looked more like he was about to lose his dinner. He turned his back to her and lowered his voice to a whisper. "And just what am I supposed to do with Faith Broderick in the meantime?"

The old man laughed. "Now, boy, if you don't know what to do with a purty woman on a deserted ranch, there ain't no hope for you."

The cell phone began to beep, signaling the battery was about to go dead. "Whiskers, you've got my truck and we're twenty miles from the Rocking M," Cooper said, starting to realize the gravity of what the old geezer had done. Careful to keep his voice low, he asked, "What the hell are we supposed to do for food?"

"I've already seen to that." Whiskers sounded so damned proud of himself that Cooper wanted to reach through the phone and shake him. "Everything you two are gonna need is already inside the house or the barn. I even seen to puttin' your clothes in there 'fore I left.''

"But there's no electricity." Cooper hated sounding desperate, but the battery on the cell phone wouldn't last for more than a few seconds longer and Whiskers knew damned good and well there was no way to charge it.

"You don't need 'lectricity, boy," Whiskers said, laughing. "Now, treat that little gal like the lady she is and I'll see you in a week."

Before Cooper had a chance to say anything more, the cell phone went completely silent. He looked at the display screen. Nothing. He slowly snapped the useless apparatus shut and barely resisted the urge to throw it as far as he possibly could.

Instead he clipped it to his belt and reviewed the facts. He was stuck on a deserted ranch with a woman he didn't know, had no transportation and no means of communication. He turned to face her. And worst of all, he had to break the news of their situation to her.

If Cooper could have gotten his hands on Whiskers at that very moment, he'd have cheerfully choked the stuffing out of the meddling old goat.

Faith watched Cooper Adams turn to face her. He didn't look at all happy. "Is something wrong?" she asked, apprehension forming a tight knot in her stomach.

He shifted from one foot to the other, then removed his cowboy hat to run a hand through his thick, dark blond hair. He stared off into the distance as if he couldn't quite meet her questioning gaze.

Placing his hat back on his head, he finally faced her. "Uh…it seems that we might have a slight problem."

The knot in Faith's stomach clenched even tighter and her knees began to tremble. Cooper clearly had something he didn't want to tell her and, if the expression on his handsome face was any indication of what was running through his mind, she wasn't going to like hearing what he had to say.

She walked over to the pile of luggage and sat down on one of the larger suitcases before her trembling legs failed her completely. "What is it?"

His broad chest expanded as he took a deep breath. "It seems Whiskers has decided to stay up at my sister and brother-in-law's ranch. He won't be returning until Flint gets back from vacation and brings my cattle over from the Rocking M."

Faith felt a tension headache coming on. Although she wasn't from Texas, she'd read enough to know that some ranches were spread out over several hundreds, sometimes thousands of acres, and were miles apart.

"When will that be?" she asked, feeling her life begin to spin out of control.

He ran a hand over his face before his bluer-than-sin gaze met hers. "In about a week."

Her heart skipped several beats. Not good. Not good at all. "If you would be kind enough to take me to Amarillo, I'll…"

She'd what? There was nothing for her there, nor was there anything for her back in Illinois. Nothing but small town gossip and the constant reminder of all her failings. Her head began to pound. How could her carefully laid plans have taken such a wrong turn?

"Ms. Broderick, that's the biggest part of our problem," Cooper said, breaking into her thoughts. "When Whiskers drove off in my truck, he took our only means of transportation with him."

Faith looked around. There wasn't a vehicle in sight. Not even a tractor. She glanced at the cell phone clipped to Cooper's belt. "Use your phone to call someone. I'm sure Mr. West would—"

"The battery's dead."

She gulped. "Then charge it."

He shook his head. "Can't. The electricity hasn't been turned on."

Her head pounded harder. "You mean we're stuck here for the next week with no way to leave and no means of communication?"

He nodded, his grim expression verifying her fears. "That's exactly what I mean."

Faith swallowed her rising panic and rubbed her throbbing temples with her fingertips. Why had Mr. Penn lied to her about owning the ranch? And why had he stranded her here with the sexiest cowboy she'd ever seen?

Whiskers Penn and her late grandfather had been friends since they were boys, and when her grandmother told Faith about the job, she'd vouched for his integrity. That's why Faith had contacted him and taken the position. Whiskers had her grandmother's approval—not an easy thing to obtain—and it had seemed an easy way to leave the past behind and start rebuilding her life.

But in her haste to do that, she'd apparently repeated her mistake. She'd trusted in basic goodness and honesty. She'd been so desperate to make a fresh start that she'd jumped from one bad situation to another. And once again, she'd been burned. Would she never learn that she had to stop trusting people and taking everything they said as the truth?

Disgusted with herself for once again being so gullible, she asked, "Why would Mr. Penn do something like this?"

"Because the old geezer has a streak of mischief in him a mile wide," Cooper muttered. He folded his arms across his wide chest. "Whether we like it or not, Ms. Broderick, we're both going to have to get used to the idea of being stuck here for the next week."

Cooper glanced at his new home, then back at Faith. The place was way too small for his peace of mind. Hell, every time they turned around they'd be bumping into each other. The thought of his body brushing against hers sent a flash of heat straight to his loins.

Shaking his head to clear it, he swept his hand toward the house. "We might as well go see what the inside looks like."

She gave him one of those you're-feeding-me-a-line looks, before asking, "If what you say is true— if this place does belong to you—then why don't you know what the interior of your own home looks like?"

He sighed heavily. "Because I was fool enough to buy it, sight unseen."

"Why would you do that?" she asked, skepticism written all over her pretty face. "Even I'm not *that* gullible."

Cooper shook his head. He'd asked himself the

same thing about a hundred times in the last half hour. "After I retired from bullriding, I started doing commentary for a few rodeo companies. But I'm tired of living like a nomad. When I made the decision to find a place to settle down, I was out on the circuit and didn't have time to get back before the auction. And Flint and my sister were away at a horse show."

"So you had Whiskers make the bid?" she guessed.

He nodded. "Unfortunately, I trusted Whiskers when he said it needed a little work, but that it was a good deal." Cooper blew out a disgusted breath. "You can bet I won't make *that* mistake again."

She glanced at the bags around her, then rose from her perch atop one of the biggest suitcases he'd ever seen. Why was it that men could stuff everything they'd need for a month in a single duffel bag, but women needed at least a six-piece set of luggage for an overnight stay?

"I suppose it would be a good idea to start moving my things," she said, grabbing a suitcase in each hand. "It looks like it's going to start raining any minute."

Cooper glanced up at the clouds building overhead, then at the monstrous pile of luggage. Hefting as many bags as he could carry at one time, he started for the house. If they hurried, they might get everything transferred to shelter before the sky opened up and poured.

Fat raindrops suddenly began to raise little puffs of dust as they hit the dusty soil.

Then again, maybe they wouldn't, he decided as they jogged toward the house. By the time they covered the distance to the sagging porch, water was coming down in sheets and, instead of soaking into the ground, it started to form little rivulets of mud.

Dropping the load in front of the door, Cooper turned and sprinted back to what remained of the pile. Scooping up the last three bags, he ran through the downpour and up the porch steps, careful to avoid cracking his head on the sagging eaves of the roof.

Faith had already entered the house, which was fine with him. The sight of her cute little backside bobbing as she ran to the shelter of the porch had already sent his blood pressure up about fifty points and activated his imagination more than he was comfortable with. Considering their situation, having his thoughts stray in an erotic direction was pure insanity.

As he stood there trying to figure out how they'd get through the next week without him walking around in a constant state of arousal, a crash, followed by a woman's bloodcurdling scream brought him back to his senses. The sound sent a chill straight up his spine and made the hair on the back of his neck stand on end.

"What the hell?"

The old wooden screen door suddenly flew open and before Cooper knew what was happening, Faith Broderick came flying out, vaulted the pile of luggage and wrapped herself around him tighter than a piece of shrink-wrap on a hot plate.

Two

Faith felt Cooper's arms close protectively around her a moment before he stumbled back down the steps to sit down hard in the muddy yard. Instantly drenched by the pouring rain, she parted the wet waves of her hair to find their faces only inches apart.

Time stood still as she sat on his lap, straddling his lean hips, feeling the rock hardness of his thighs beneath her bottom. Staring at him, she felt she just might drown in his deep blue eyes. His firm lips parted and she wondered how they would feel on her own. Would they be hard and demanding, or gentle and coaxing?

Despite the chilling rain beating down on her, Faith felt an inner heat warm her all the way to her toes. Even soaking wet the man was gorgeous and made her think of things she had no business dwelling on. And that wasn't good, considering for the next week they would be stranded together on a deserted ranch.

"Are you all right?" he finally asked, his voice sounding so darned intimate and sexy that her temperature rose another couple of notches.

His face was so close she could feel his warm breath on her cheek, see the tiny scar just below his right eyebrow that she hadn't noticed before. His arms held her securely against his broad chest and the feel of his body pressed to her sensitive breasts made her insides feel as if they'd turned to pudding.

Not at all comfortable with the feeling, she scrambled to her feet. "I, uh…yes. Yes, I'm fine." She hated her breathless tone and the fact that her knees didn't want to support her.

Water dripped from his tan cowboy hat as for several long seconds they continued to stare wordlessly at each other. "Come on," he finally said. Rising to his feet, he took her by the hand to tug her along. "Let's get out of this rain."

Faith had forgotten all about the downpour and the fact that they were both soaking wet. She'd been too fascinated by the sight of his soaked western shirt molded to his perfect torso and broad shoulders. Her ex-husband had worked out at the gym for years and never managed to build the type of rock hard muscles that Cooper Adams had. But then, she'd learned the hard way that Eric hadn't spent as much time at the gym as she'd been led to believe.

Back under the shelter of the sagging porch roof, she noticed Cooper's eyes darken to pools of navy as he stared at her. When she realized the exact direction of his gaze, Faith quickly crossed her arms over her breasts, her cheeks burning. Thoroughly drenched, her pale yellow T-shirt might as well have been transparent. It clung to her breasts like a second skin and her flimsy lace bra left little or nothing to the imagination. A fact that Cooper seemed to find quite fascinating.

He cleared his throat. "What the hell happened in there?" he finally asked.

It took her a moment to realize what he meant. Remembering the reason for her flight from the house, she shuddered. "There's some kind of hideous creature in the kitchen."

He sighed heavily. "What did it look like?"

"Well, I...I don't know exactly," Faith admitted.

"You didn't see it?"

She shook her head. "I didn't stick around long enough to find out how horrible it looked."

He propped his hands on his hips and stared down at her. "Then what makes you think it was horrible?"

"Because when I knocked over a box full of pans it made an awful hissing sound." Irritated by Cooper's questions and the amusement dancing in his eyes, she glared at him. "I wasn't about to stand there and let it bite me."

His lips twitched, and she had no doubt he was trying to keep from laughing out loud. She wanted to punch him. Why did men feel so darned superior when it came to a woman's fears of creepy things?

"Well, we can do one of two things," he said solicitously.

She glared at him. "And what would that be, Mr. Adams?"

"We can either stand here and debate the issue while we freeze our butts off in these wet clothes, or we can go inside and change.'' He shrugged and reached for the screen door. "I'm opting for warm and dry. How about you?''

The temperature had to have dropped a good ten degrees with the onset of the rain and the October breeze had picked up enough to blow water in from the open side of the porch. ''But what about...the animal...in there?'' Faith asked, her teeth beginning to chatter. She wasn't about to go back inside the house until the creature had been dealt with.

He let go a long, resigned sigh. "Where did you see the damned thing?''

"I told you...I didn't see it. I only *heard* it.''

He rolled his eyes. "Okay. Where did you *hear* this hideous beast?''

"In...the kitchen,'' she said, shivering as much from the memory of the sound, as from her wet clothing. ''By...the boxes in the center...of the room.''

Cooper opened the door and stepped into the dim light of the kitchen. In truth, he was damned glad to put some distance between himself and Faith Broderick. When she'd come flying out of the house and jumped into his arms, the feel of her soft body clinging to him, her long legs wrapped around his waist, had just about sent his blood pressure into stroke range. But it was the sight of her wet T-shirt that had almost done him in completely. He'd been left with more than a clear image of the size and shape of her breasts, and when her nipples tightened from the chilled air, his eyes had damned near popped out of his head. How was a man supposed to ignore a sight like that? Or forget about it?

He shook his head. He couldn't do either. And he

had a feeling the next week was going to be sheer hell.

Glancing around, he decided whatever Faith had heard must have moved on. As he turned to tell her the coast was clear, a movement on top of the boxes in the center of the room caught his attention. He stepped closer and the little lizard let loose with a loud hiss.

As frustrating as their situation was, Cooper couldn't help but chuckle at the turn of events and his own foolishness. When he'd first laid eyes on Faith, he'd thought he might like to move a mountain or slay a dragon for her. It appeared he'd get to do both. He'd already moved that mountainous pile of luggage, now he'd get to play the white knight and get rid of her dragon.

You've got to get out more, Adams.

When a man started suffering the "white knight" syndrome over a lizard and a pile of beat-up suitcases, it was a sure sign he'd been too long without the warmth of a woman.

"Here's your 'hideous creature,'" he said, pushing open the screen door.

"What is that thing?" she asked, drawing back as he walked past her to the edge of the porch.

"It's just a little old horny toad." He released the reptile, then turned to face her. "He didn't mean any harm."

"I...I'll have...to take...your word...for that," she said, shivering violently.

She had to be chilled to the bone and damned uncomfortable in those wet clothes. Stopping himself from wrapping her in his arms, he reached for the screen door instead. They were little more than strangers and he had a feeling she wouldn't buy that he was trying to lend her his warmth any more than he would.

Placing his hand at her back, Cooper ushered her through the door, then quickly put distance between them before he did something stupid. "Where do you want me to put your bags?" he asked, preparing to relocate Mount Samsonite to its next location.

"Put them in…the living room for now," she said, shivering as she looked around the kitchen. "Before I start unpacking anything…we'll have to clean."

Cooper took that to mean she intended for him to do a critter check of the house and get rid of any more unwanted guests.

Once her suitcases had been moved and he'd located the duffels Whiskers had left for him, Cooper retrieved a couple of towels. Walking back into the kitchen, he handed her one of the plush bath sheets. "You'd better get dried off and put on something warm."

She eyed him warily.

All things considered, he guessed he could understand her reluctance to strip down even with him in one room and her in another. She had no way of knowing he could be trusted not to violate her privacy, or that he was about as harmless as that little lizard he'd pitched out earlier.

Wanting to put her mind at ease, he squarely met her uncertain gaze. "You don't have to be afraid of me, Faith. You've got my word, I'll stay in here while you change."

The sound of his deep baritone saying her name sent a shiver up Faith's spine and had her scurrying into the living room to find dry clothes. Cooper might not think of himself as the threatening type, but she knew better. Physically, she had no doubt he would keep his promise. How she knew that, she wasn't sure. She just did.

But the fact that he practically oozed virility from every pore of his skin was what had her concerned. She didn't want to find Cooper Adams attractive, didn't want to think of him as honorable or trustworthy. In fact, she didn't want to think of him at all. Her peace of mind depended on it.

But the memory of his body pressed to hers, the smell of his clean masculine skin and the integrity she'd detected in his deep blue eyes wouldn't allow her to forget.

She peeled her wet clothes off and vigorously ran the towel over her skin in an effort to rub away a fresh wave of goose bumps that had nothing to do with being chilled, and everything to do with thinking about Cooper Adams.

Faith selected a black sweatshirt and matching sweatpants from one of her suitcases. Certain her choice would be as appealing to a man as a burlap bag, she pulled them on, along with a pair of thick socks. Digging around in the suitcase containing her shoes, she slipped on a pair of cross trainers, combed the damp waves of her hair into a semblance of order, then ventured back into the kitchen.

"At least Whiskers brought something to heat the house with," Cooper said, looking up as she entered the room. He finished lighting a large kerosene heater, then straightened and started unbuttoning his shirt. "I'll change, then help you go through the boxes to see what kind of food the old geezer left for us."

She nodded. She couldn't do anything else. As he parted the front of the garment, the sight of well-defined ridges on his stomach and perfectly sculpted pectoral muscles struck her completely speechless. He pulled the sleeves from his arms and she swallowed hard. His biceps were moving in really fascinating ways as he shrugged out of the shirt. She remembered how securely those arms had held her to keep her from being injured when they landed in the yard and how safe she'd felt with them wrapped around her.

Oblivious to what the sight of all that masculine flesh and sinew was doing to her, he turned and headed for the living room. A long white scar ran down from just below his shoulder blade to curve around his left side, but it didn't even come close to detracting from the sexiness of his broad shoulders and narrow waist. But when she noticed his tight rear encased in those well-worn jeans, Faith caught her breath. Lord have mercy, except for the scar, the man's body was absolutely perfect.

She shook her head to chase away her foolishness. He was nothing more than a good-looking, well-built man. And she'd learned the hard way that men couldn't be counted on for anything but a truckload of grief.

If she intended to get through the next week with any sanity left, she'd have to remember that. She'd also have to keep her gaze from straying anywhere below Cooper's chin, in order to avoid panting over his gorgeous body.

As soon as he entered the living room, Cooper blew out the air trapped in his lungs and ran a hand over his abdomen. He'd never had a problem with a bulging stomach. But when he'd noticed Faith staring at him like a hungry dog after a juicy steak, he'd damned near suffocated trying to tighten his already flat belly.

What the hell had gotten into him? He'd never in his life felt the need to impress a woman with his physique. He hadn't needed to. From about the age of fifteen he'd pretty much had all the female attention he wanted or—for that matter—could handle.

He frowned. It had to have been a case of temporary insanity. That's all it could be. He'd been working so hard lately, he hadn't had the time to think about a woman, let alone be with one. And finding himself stranded on a deserted ranch with a beautiful female after a long dry spell wasn't going to make the next several days any easier. Not by a long shot.

Satisfied that he'd discovered the reason for his irrational behavior, Cooper shucked his muddy jeans and toweled himself dry. He could tell she didn't like the attraction any better than he did. But that didn't change the fact that it was there. They just had to ignore it.

That might be easier said than done, though. Faith had put on a sweat suit, and Cooper would bet his last dollar it was an attempt to lessen her appeal. He chuckled. She had no idea that even if it was baggy fleece, she made black look good. Real good.

When his body reminded him of the way she'd felt sitting on his lap, he shook his head. That line of thinking was not going to help the situation one damned bit.

Pulling on a dry set of clothes, he forced himself

to look around his new home. If anything could douse a case of the hots and get his mind back on track, it was all the work he had ahead of him. Cooper wandered into one of the three bedrooms and discovered that he'd get a lot of the repairs done while they were stranded.

Whiskers had planned quite well and thought of just about everything. New panes of glass for the broken windows were propped against the walls awaiting installation, gallon buckets of paint for both the inside and outside of the house were stacked in one corner and several squares of shingles to fix the roof were stacked in another. A tool belt with a hammer, tape measure and caulking gun, along with several boxes of nails and an assortment of handsaws were piled on top of a stack of plywood resting on sawhorses. Two large rolls of heavyweight plastic with a note attached rounded out the supplies.

Fencing supplies in the barn. Have a good time. Whiskers.

"Crazy old coot," Cooper muttered, relieved to find the other bedrooms had double beds with comfortable looking mattresses. At least, he'd get a good night's sleep after working himself day and night trying to get the place livable.

"Did you find candles or something we could use for light?" Faith called. He listened to her poke around in the kitchen, opening drawers and closing cabinet doors.

"I'll check," he said, grabbing a roll of plastic and the tool belt. He tucked them under his arm and walked back into the kitchen. When Faith raised a brow, he explained, "After I help you find some type of light, I'm going to tack up some of this plastic to keep the heat in and the rain from blowing through the broken windows.''

He put the tool belt and plastic to one side, opened the boxes and started pulling items out. Handing Faith a handful of candles and a camping lantern, he turned back to the cartons. ''Looks like Whiskers left us a camp stove for cooking,'' he said, setting the item on the counter.

''Tell me he left a can opener in there somewhere,'' she said, eyeing several cans. ''If he didn't, we're in bigger trouble than he is.''

''You planning on giving him a piece of your mind?'' When she nodded, Cooper laughed and held up a can opener. ''He's off the hook on this one, but you'll have to stand in line. I have first dibs on his ornery old hide.''

''How long have you known Mr. Penn?'' she asked, taking the can opener and several other kitchen utensils he'd removed from the boxes. She placed them on the counter. ''Does he do things like this very often?''

Cooper handed her a bag of rags and a spray bottle of all-purpose cleaner he'd found at the bottom of the box. ''Not really. Not since…''

His voice trailed off as he thought of the last time Whiskers had pulled a stunt like this. It had been with Cooper's sister Jenna and Flint McCray. The old geezer had purposely glossed over the news of a storm warning in order to strand them in a remote line shack. And Whiskers had even tried to get Cooper to help him. Cooper gulped as he stared at Faith's back. Jenna and Flint had just celebrated their fifth wedding anniversary.

When Whiskers called to say he was on his way

to the Rocking M, Cooper had been so angry he hadn't given much thought to the old man's reasons for stranding them. Now that he'd calmed down, Cooper knew exactly what the old goat had up his sleeve. Whiskers was trying to get them together for a trip down the aisle.

"Not since when?" Faith asked, spraying the cleaner and wiping down the insides of the cabinets with the rags.

"Not…" Cooper had to clear the gravel from his throat before he could finish speaking. "It doesn't matter. Let's just say it's been a long time and leave it at that."

She stopped cleaning and turned to look at him. "Do you think his age has something to do with his behavior?"

"Could be," Cooper hedged. "If you can handle things from here, I'm going to get this plastic put up."

When she nodded, he hastily picked up the items he needed and headed into the other room. He wasn't about to tell her that the only thing wrong with Whiskers's mind was a misguided belief that he needed to play matchmaker and see everyone he knew blissfully hitched.

Two hours later, Faith looked around to find all the boxes of food had been unpacked and put away. After Cooper had finished putting plastic over the broken windows, he'd helped her by storing the canned goods in the cabinets she'd cleaned. Then he'd tinkered with the hand pump and finally gotten enough water to warm on the camp stove for her to wash the few dishes and cooking utensils they'd found.

"Looks like Whiskers thought of just about everything," he said, pulling a blue graniteware coffeepot from one of the cartons. "At least we can start the morning off with a cup of instant daylight."

"Why do you call it that?" Faith asked, smiling at his relieved expression.

"Because one sip of my coffee and the cobwebs are instantly cleared out of your head for the rest of the day," he said proudly. "Wakes you right up and gets the blood to pumping."

Laughing, she took the pot from him and plunged it in the soapy dishwater. "It sounds a little stronger than I care for. I think I'll pass."

"Where's your sense of adventure?" he asked, grinning back.

"I lost it…" She checked her watch. "…about three hours ago."

He nodded. "I can understand. I guess it was pretty disappointing to find this place in the shape it's in." He frowned. "I know I wasn't too happy about it."

"Oh, I was just beside myself," Faith said dryly. "And then when I found out that I was going to be stranded here for the next week with no electricity it was almost more happiness than I could handle."

Cooper chuckled. "Yeah, I guess that did take care of any expectations you had about taking the job."

Faith marveled at Cooper's good-natured attitude. "But I would imagine my disillusionment pales in comparison to yours. My money didn't pay for this place. Yours did."

His grin made her feel warm all the way to her

toes. "Well, I will admit that I felt a little discouraged when I first saw it."

"A little?"

Faith could well understand how he must have felt. Her reaction upon seeing the place had been far from thrilled. But to know that your hard-earned money had gone to pay for something that needed as much work as this place did, had to have been extremely disheartening.

His laughter filled the room. "Okay. You got me on that one. I took one look and felt like I'd taken a sucker punch to the gut. But after I changed clothes, I looked through some of the rooms and it's not as bad as I first thought. There are three good-sized bedrooms, a big office and a room large enough to put in a whirlpool."

"Oh, a long soak in the tub sounds heavenly," she said, closing her eyes.

"Having inside conveniences period, would be nice," he agreed. "Especially with it raining cats and dogs."

Surely she hadn't heard him correctly. Opening her eyes, she stared at him. "Are you telling me there are *no* bathroom facilities at all?"

He nodded. "None."

She opened and closed her mouth several times as she tried to digest what he was telling her. "Then how...I mean, where are we—"

"Outside," he said, apparently aware of her concerns. "There's an outhouse about fifty yards—"

"An outhouse?!" She hated having to discuss something so intimate with a stranger, but it couldn't be helped.

He nodded. "Look, I know it's not the best of

conditions, but that doesn't mean we can't think of this as an adventure. Try pretending you're on a camping trip.''

''Right.'' She was beginning to realize just how isolated and primitive their situation was. ''Did you find a can of bug spray in any of those cartons?'' she asked suddenly.

''No.'' He looked at her like he thought she might be close to losing it. ''Why do you want bug spray?''

''Spiders.'' She shuddered. Even the word gave her the creeps and sent a chill snaking up her spine. ''I can't stand them.''

''Oh, right. I guess there might be a few that have taken up residence in there.''

''Exactly.'' There was no way she'd step foot anywhere that a spider might be lurking about just waiting to pounce on her. She shuddered. And if the spiders around here were like everything else in Texas, they'd be the size of a Volkswagen.

He walked over to the door and looked out. ''The rain's let up to a steady drizzle, but I don't think it's going to stop for a while.'' Turning back, he gave her a lopsided grin. ''I'll make you a deal. I'll go out and take care of any eight-legged varmints in there, if you'll cook supper.''

''Deal,'' Faith said, smiling back at him and extending her hand to seal the bargain.

The minute he took her hand in his, warmth streaked up her arm to spread throughout her body. His gaze caught hers and she could see by the darkening of his eyes that he'd experienced a similar reaction to their touch.

Faith jerked her hand back. ''If you'll show me how to light the stove without blowing myself up,

I'll start dinner,'' she said, hating the breathless tone of her voice.

He stood, staring at her for endless seconds before nodding and showing her how to operate the camp stove. Then, without a word, he walked out into the cool, October rain.

Three

___

Cooper watched Faith slowly push back from the makeshift table he'd constructed of plywood on sawhorses. "If you'll get 'Old Faithful' to spout forth some more water, I'll get these dishes washed," she said, sounding tired.

"Nope." Shaking his head, he got up from the crate he'd been sitting on and walked over to the pump. "You cooked. I'll take care of cleaning up."

"That's not necessary, Mr. Adams," she said, gathering their plates to stack them on the cracked countertop. "I'm used to—"

"The name's Cooper," he said, grasping the handle to see if he could coax water from the ancient pump. The first thing he intended to do when he had a means of transportation was to find the nearest hardware store and buy plumbing supplies. "You've had a hell of a day and I'm betting you're pretty tired. Besides, you fulfilled your end of the deal. You cooked.''

"But the agreement—"

"I know what the deal was," he said, pouring rain water he'd collected in a bucket into the apparatus to prime it. It had to be the ultimate irony that you had to have water to get water from old hand pumps, he decided as he moved the metal lever up and down several times until water finally belched forth from "Old Faithful." Filling a large pot, he set it on the camp stove and lit the burner before turning to face her.

The combination of fatigue and nerves had taken their toll. She'd yawned several times in the last half hour and a hint of dark circles had appeared under her beautiful brown eyes.

"Where did you say you're from?"

"Illinois." She covered her mouth against another yawn.

"When was the last time you slept?"

"Night before last." She yawned again. "I was too excited about the trip to sleep last night."

He whistled low. "You have to be dead on your feet. Why don't you get ready and go to bed? While you finished cooking supper, I found some sheets and made both beds. All you have to do is crawl in and crash."

"But—"

"But nothing." Cooper placed his hands on her shoulders and turned her away from the counter. He quickly turned her loose and did his best to ignore the heated sensation running from his palms, up his arms and gathering in his gut. "Get some rest."

He watched her eye the door. "Is it still raining?"

"No."

"Did Whiskers leave a flashlight?"

"Yes, but why do you—" When she jerked her thumb in the direction of the outhouse, understanding dawned. "Oh, yeah. Sorry."

Handing her the requested light, he busied himself with the dishes as she quietly opened the door and stepped outside. Why did he feel the need to shelter this woman? What was there about Faith Broderick that made him want to take care of her?

Several times throughout the afternoon and evening he'd detected a quiet reserve about her, a sadness she couldn't quite hide. Maybe that was why he'd felt his protective instinct rear its head.

He'd developed that particular trait when he'd been responsible for watching out for his sister, Jenna. After their mother abandoned the family for greener pastures, their dad had lost interest in life, leaving Cooper with no choice but to finish raising himself and his sister. But he'd learned to tamp down any more of his sheltering tendencies with other women. Jenna had pointed out time and again that he tended to be on the overly protective side, and that women didn't particularly care for that these days.

Nope. He wasn't going to get involved or try to help Faith with whatever bothered her. She'd probably tell him to mind his own business anyway.

The back door suddenly flew open, breaking into his thoughts. White as a sheet and trembling uncontrollably, Faith slammed the door and leaned back against it.

"What's wrong?" he asked, rushing over to her. He could tell something had terrified her and without a second thought, he wrapped her in his arms. So much for his internal pep talk.

Sagging against him, she shook her head. "I'm not going back out there."

"Why? What happened?"

"Didn't you hear it?" she asked, her voice shaky.

"Hear what?"

She pushed back from his chest to meet his gaze. "Something out there is howling like a wounded banshee."

Confused, Cooper stared down at her. "I didn't hear…" He stopped in midsentence. He had heard something, but he was so used to it, the sound hadn't really registered. "Coyote," he said, hoping his smile reflected reassurance instead of the physical awareness streaking through his body. "That was just an old coyote yipping at the moon. He didn't—"

"Don't tell me. I know. He didn't mean any harm." She pushed from his embrace. "The creatures I've encountered so far might not mean to hurt me, but they've certainly succeeded in scaring the living daylights out of me."

He let her go. She'd felt way too good nestled against him. And that wasn't going to make the next week any easier. No siree.

She stood for a moment, staring at the door, then turned to walk into the living room. Realizing she hadn't had time to reach her outdoor destination, he tried to think of the least embarrassing way to offer his assistance.

"I'm going that way," he said, taking the flashlight from her. He was proud of himself for managing to sound nonchalant. "Want to tag along?"

A blush tinted her pale cheeks, but after a moment's hesitation, she nodded.

Ten minutes later, Faith stepped back onto the porch. She truly appreciated Cooper's consideration for her privacy when they'd reached the outhouse. He'd stood several yards away, making her feel a little better about his accompanying her. But not much.

She was still embarrassed beyond words over her recent behavior. Normally she took things in stride and let very little frighten her. Hadn't her ex-husband always called her the strong one in their relationship—The Rock?

The only explanation she could think of for her uncharacteristic fear had to be exhaustion. And not just from the trip to the ranch, or the disillusionment she'd felt at finding herself stranded here with the sexiest man she'd ever seen.

No, it had more to do with the emotionally draining events of the past year than anything else. She wished she had a nickel for every piece of small-town gossip and all the instances of humiliation she'd suffered when everybody in the community learned that her husband had left her to marry her best friend. If she did, she'd be a very rich woman and wouldn't be seeking employment on a run-down ranch in the Texas Panhandle.

But she'd lived through it, held her head high and ignored as much of it as she could. Only her grandmother knew the true extent of how badly she'd been hurt by her husband and *former* best friend.

Faith shook her head and put it out of her mind. Now was the time to move forward, not to look back.

No one here knew the circumstances surrounding her divorce, or that her judgment had been seriously flawed. As far as she was concerned, they'd never find out either.

Taking the battery operated lantern from the middle of the plywood table, she walked into the living room and eyed her suitcases. "Have you decided which bedroom you're taking?"

"Doesn't matter to me," Cooper said, following her into the room. He pushed his hat back on his head, then jammed his hands in the front pockets of his jeans as he rocked back on his heels. "Take the one you want and I'll take what's left. I'll move your luggage in the morning."

"All right."

She gathered her nightgown, slippers and robe into one arm, traded him the lantern for the flashlight and walked down the short hall to enter the first bedroom she came to. Stopping short as the beam of light flashed across the bed, she bit her lip to keep a hysterical giggle from escaping. Life just kept getting more bizarre with each passing minute.

Leaning back around the door, she called, "Uh...Cooper, we have a slight problem."

"What's wrong? Did you see another critter? I swear I checked—"

"No." She couldn't keep from laughing. It was just too unreal to be believed. "I think this problem is a lot bigger."

"What makes you think that?" he asked, walking toward her with the lantern. The light cast his features into sharp relief and accented the frown furrowing his brow. He was the best-looking man she'd seen in years. Maybe ever.

Shaking her head to dispel the wayward thought, she pointed into the room. "Unless I'm mistaken, that's chunks of the ceiling on top of my bed."

Shouldering past her, he raised the lantern to get a better look. Pieces of plaster and dust covered the entire double bed. He suddenly let loose with a string of curses that all but turned the air blue and ended with a threat to do bodily harm to Whiskers Penn.

When he stopped cursing, he looked thoroughly disgusted. "The roof must have leaked, water collected behind the plaster—"

"And it gave way," Faith finished for him, unable to stop giggling.

He eyed her like she might be suffering from hysteria. "Do you feel all right?" he finally asked, ushering her into the bedroom that would have been his. "Maybe you should lie down."

Nodding, she wiped the tears at the corners of her eyes. "I'm fine, but this whole day has been a disaster."

He stared at her a moment longer, then threw back his head and laughed with her. "It has been like something out of a bad movie, hasn't it?"

"So what do we do now?" she asked, yawning.

"Nothing." He sat down on the side of the bed and took off his boots.

What on earth was the man up to? she wondered.

Cooper stood up in the middle of the bed and poked at the ceiling. "This one's fine," he said, stepping back down on the floor. "No signs of weakness, so you should be safe from any more falling plaster. You take this bed and I'll bunk down in the living room."

"But—"

"Don't argue." He walked to the door. "You need sleep," he said, his low sexy drawl sounding like a caress. "Good night."

"Nite."

In the silence that followed the quiet click of the door, Faith felt the last traces of her energy drain away. Her arms and legs suddenly felt like lead weights and she was too tired to think about this latest turn of events, let alone how to deal with it.

Slowly changing into her nightgown, she crawled between the cool sheets. She tried to free her mind and forget everything about the entire day. But as soon as she closed her eyes, a tall, sexy Texan with eyes bluer-than-sin and a voice that made her feel all warm and fuzzy inside, filled her mind and beckoned her into the welcome respite of sleep.

Cooper whistled an off-key version of a popular Garth Brooks song while he propped the ladder against the side of the house. He hoped like hell the ladder didn't sink in the mud. But while there was a break in the weather, he needed to get plastic on the east side of the roof. He'd much rather be slapping shingles in place, but the way the clouds were gathering up in the northwest, he'd be lucky to get the sheeting nailed in place before the sky opened up and poured again.

Once he climbed onto the roof, he quickly unrolled the plastic and began nailing it down. Halfway through the task he realized someone was calling his name. Peering over the edge of the roof, he spotted Faith standing with her doubled fists propped on her shapely hips, a scowl on her pretty face. She'd pulled on the baggy black sweat suit and it looked as if a lover's hands had been tangled in her long auburn hair. He didn't think he'd ever seen a woman look quite so sexy.

"Morning," he said, grinning down at her.

"What in all that's holy do you think you're doing?" she demanded, her voice still husky from sleep.

"Fixing the roof."

She didn't smile back. "What time is it?"

Cooper checked his watch. "It's a little past seven. I could tell how tired you were last night. That's why I didn't wake you for breakfast. I thought I'd let you sleep in."

"And just how did you think I'd be able to sleep with you banging on the roof above my head?" she asked, giving him a look that clearly stated she didn't think he had enough sense to pour water out of a boot with the directions on the heel.

"Uh, sorry about that." He ran his hand across the back of his neck. He hadn't even thought about waking her. "I'm used to Whiskers being around. He can sleep through anything. And I wanted to get this plastic on before it rained again."

Fat raindrops began to make little plopping noises on the heavy plastic and the wind suddenly picked up. The end of the sheeting he hadn't yet tacked down began to flap wildly. Cooper lunged to keep the wind from tearing loose the end he'd already nailed in place. In the process, he lost his grip on the hammer. He watched it slide down the roof, then heard it drop to the soft dirt below.

"Damn," he muttered. How was he going to hold the plastic and climb down for the hammer?

"Lose something?" Faith asked.

Her voice sounded close. Too close.

He glanced over his shoulder and his heart came up in his throat. She'd just finished climbing the ladder and was crawling on all fours up the slope of the roof toward him.

"What the hell do you think you're doing, lady?" he demanded, holding his breath until she was sprawled out on top of the plastic beside him. She was afraid of harmless critters, but she'd scaled a ladder to lend him a hand? Maybe she was more gutsy than he'd first thought. "You could fall and break your neck."

"You're very welcome, Mr. Adams," she said, handing him the hammer. "Now hush and get this thing nailed down while I hold it. I'd like to get off the roof before we both get soaked."

Taking the tool from her, Cooper quickly nailed the sheeting. "Okay, it's done," he said, pounding the last nail into place. "Thanks."

"No problem." She sat up and began to make her way toward the ladder, but hadn't gone more than a few inches before she started sliding on the wet plastic. "Ooh…"

Cooper quickly reached out, circled her waist with his arm and hauled her to him. "Careful, darlin'. We'll have to take this slow or we'll both wind up flat on our backs on the ground."

He closed his eyes and took a deep breath. His heart felt as if it was in his throat as he held her close. What would have happened if he hadn't been able to catch her before she slid down the slope of the roof? With no transportation and no way to call for help, it could have been disastrous.

The heat of her slender body pressed to his chest,

the feel of her breasts resting on his forearm and the scent of her peach shampoo where her hair tickled his nose, quickly turned his thoughts from what had almost happened to what he'd like to have happen.

Cooper suddenly felt as if he'd already taken a dive off the roof and landed on his head. Damn but the woman smelled good. Felt good in his arms.

"What do we do now?" she asked, sounding breathless.

He threw the hammer over the side of the roof, shifted her to sit between his thighs, then wrapped both of his arms around her middle. "We're going to take this real slow and scoot our way over to the ladder."

He felt her spine stiffen at the intimate contact of her bottom resting so intimately against the most vulnerable part of him, but placing her hands on his forearms, she nodded.

Slowly, carefully maneuvering them toward the ladder, Cooper felt his lower body awaken to the fact that a delectable, feminine rear was rubbing against it. His problem must have registered with her, too, because she stopped scooting to glare at him over her shoulder.

"Mr. Adams—"

"I don't like it any more than you do," he lied, interrupting what he figured to be a strongly worded warning. He wasn't about to tell her that he was having a hell of a time fighting the urge to throw caution to the wind and seduce her right here on the roof. She'd probably throw him over the side herself if she found out.

"There's nothing I can do about it," he tried explaining. "You're a beautiful woman and I'm a flesh and blood man, not a damned saint."

Faith's cheeks burned. It seemed that every time she turned around she found herself in Cooper's arms. How on earth did she manage to get herself into these predicaments anyway? More than that, why was her body responding to his?

As soon as he'd caught her from sliding off the roof, tiny currents of electrical impulses had streaked through her to form a coil deep in the pit of her stomach. The feel of his changing body pressed to her backside tightened the coil and reminded her that she hadn't been held by a man, loved by a man, for well over a year.

Giving herself a mental shake, she took a deep breath in hopes of steadying her voice and nerves. "Let's just get down from here and out of this rain."

"Works for me," he said, tightening his hold on her and carefully scooting them both toward the edge of the roof. Reaching their destination, he lifted her to lie beside him. "I'm going down first. If you slip on the wet rungs, I'll be there to catch you." He lifted his hand to brush her cheek with his knuckles. "I promise I won't let you get hurt."

His statement set off alarm bells deep within her soul. But his warm breath feathering over her cheek, sent shivers of excitement down her spine. She watched his blue gaze darken to navy and his lips part as he stared down at her. The warning signals seemed to fade considerably.

"I want to kiss you," he said simply.

"That wouldn't be wise."

He shook his head. "Probably not. Would you stop me if I did?"

The alarm bells went completely silent, and instead of nodding that she would stop him, she shook her head.

"Do you want me to kiss you, Faith?"

"Yes."

Yes? Had she lost the last of what little sense she had left? They were stretched out on a rooftop, it was raining buckets and she'd just told him she wanted his kiss.

Faith watched Cooper push his hat back, then slowly, deliberately move closer. She could tell he was giving her the chance to change her mind, to call a halt to this insanity. But she found she really did want his kiss, wanted to feel his firm lips pressed to hers, wanted to know the taste of him.

Her breath caught and she closed her eyes as his mouth descended to hers. Warm, firm and oh so exciting, the contact caused sparkles of light to flash behind her closed lids and she felt as if the roof shifted beneath her.

Cooper coaxed her to open for him and she couldn't have stopped herself if her life depended on it. She wanted his kiss, wanted to feel his tongue mate with hers. Heaven help her, but it had been so very long since she'd tasted a man's desire, felt his body respond to hers.

He slid his hand from her hip, beneath the tail of her sweatshirt and up her ribs to the swell of her breast. Cupping the weight with his large hand, he teased the hardened tip with his thumb. "You're not wearing a bra."

"I...didn't have time...to put one on," she said, her head spinning from the sensations his touch created.

"I'm glad," he said huskily.

His callused palm felt absolutely wonderful on her sensitized skin and she couldn't stop a small moan from escaping. The long forgotten sound of her own passion startled her. What in the name of heaven was she doing? Had she completely lost her mind?

She had to spend the next week with this man. Falling into his arms, welcoming his kiss, spelled disaster at any time. But the day after her arrival? It was pure insanity.

"Please let me go," she said, pushing against his chest.

He allowed her to sit up, but didn't let go of her arms. "Don't be upset, darlin'. A little kiss among friends never hurt anyone."

Faith felt as if she'd been dumped into a tub of ice water. She knew better than anyone how deadly a kiss among friends could be, how it could destroy lives. Two years ago, her husband's affair with her best friend had started with a friendly little kiss under the mistletoe at the staff Christmas party where they all worked.

Cooper had said that he wouldn't let her get hurt and she had no doubt he would keep her safe physically. But there were other types of hurt. She had firsthand knowledge of how emotional pain lasted longer and left deeper scars than any physical injury ever could.

The warning signals were practically screaming at her to run as hard and fast as she could. To put as much distance as possible between herself and Cooper Adams.

Pulling from his grasp, Faith scooted herself to the ladder and began her descent to the ground. She had a feeling he was completely unaware of the effect he had on women, of how his very presence charged the atmosphere with enough electricity to light a small city. The fact that he'd turned that energy her way, scared her to death.

"Faith, wait a minute," she heard him call from above.

She ignored his request and continued to scurry down the ladder. She needed to put distance between them. She had to get her equilibrium back.

No sooner had she thought of regaining her mental balance, than her foot slipped on the wet rung and she fell the last few feet to the ground. She landed hard on her right foot, but ignoring the numb, cold feeling that followed, she started for the house. She'd only taken a couple of steps when a searing pain shot through her ankle and up her calf. Crying out, she stumbled and would have fallen if not for the two strong arms scooping her up and cradling her to a wide chest.

She gazed at the man holding her. Cooper's bluer-than-sin eyes were filled with nothing but kindness and concern.

Tears blurred her vision and she buried her face in the side of his neck. Would she never stop making a fool of herself in front of this man?

Four

When Cooper scooped Faith into his arms, she pressed her face to the side of his neck and her shoulders shook with silent sobs. It just about tore him apart.

She'd scared the living hell out of him when she'd jerked from his arms and started down the ladder. Visions of her falling and being seriously injured had flashed through his mind and he'd immediately started down after her. But when she fell, he'd swear he aged a good ten years.

Any way he looked at it, he was responsible for her falling. He'd known how jumpy she'd become after feeling his body respond to hers. But like a damned fool, he'd reacted with his hormones instead of his good sense. He'd given into the temptation that had eaten at him since he first watched her get out of Bubba's truck. And she'd gotten hurt because of it.

"It's going to be okay, darlin'," he said, shouldering open the kitchen door.

"Please put me down."

"No."

"I can walk," she insisted. Her warm breath on the side of his neck caused him to clench his jaw so tight he thought he'd most likely crack a couple of teeth.

She might be able to walk, but Cooper wasn't real positive that he could for all that much longer. "Are you sure?" he asked.

When she nodded, her silky hair brushed the side of his jaw. His blood pressure shot up several points and his lungs refused to take in air.

Setting her on her feet, he asked, "Are you certain you're okay?"

"Yes." She started to limp toward the living room, but in her haste she bumped into the edge of their makeshift table.

Cooper caught her before she fell and swung her up into his arms once again. She pressed her face to his shoulder and Cooper felt every one of his protective instincts spring to life, as well as every one of his hormones.

Heading straight for the bedroom she'd used the night before, he gently placed her on the rumpled sheets. He tried not to think about how her slender body had felt pressed to his chest, or how much he'd like to crawl into bed next to her, take her into his arms and...

Stepping away from the bed, he started backing his way out of the room. "I'll be right back."

"Don't bother," she said, throwing her arm across her eyes. "I'd rather die by myself."

Apprehension tightened his gut. He hadn't thought she'd been injured *that* seriously. "Die? I thought you said—"

"Of humiliation," she said, sounding disgusted.

Cooper was relieved to hear her sense of humor had returned. "You're embarrassed?"

She nodded, but kept her eyes covered with her arm. "You probably won't believe this, but I'm normally a very sensible, very 'together' person." She paused to take a deep, steadying breath. "And I'm never clumsy."

"Never?"

She lifted her arm to glare at him. "Never."

Cooper wisely suppressed his smile. At least her spirit was intact. "I'm going to get the first-aid kit. I'll be right back."

Turning, he retraced his steps to the living room to rummage through one of the duffel bags Whiskers had left for him. When he found the white metal box filled with medical supplies he always carried, he returned to the bedroom and sat down on the bed beside her.

"Let's get this shoe off and see what we've got here," he said, carefully lifting her leg to rest it on his knee.

He pushed the bottom of her sweatpants up to midcalf and tried not to notice the feel of her satiny skin beneath his palm. Now was not the time for a case of the hots, he reminded himself. That was what had gotten them into this mess in the first place. If he hadn't acted like a seventeen-year-old with a perpetual hard-on and scared the hell out of her, she wouldn't have been injured.

Easing the cross-trainer from her foot, he carefully peeled the sock off and examined her ankle. He was relieved that there was very little swelling. He'd seen enough injuries in his many years on the rodeo circuit to tell that it was most likely a mild sprain and not broken.

"Can you wiggle your toes without pain?" he asked, running his hands over the delicate bones on the top of her foot.

She moved them without hesitation. "I'm fine. Now, go away, Adams."

He chuckled. "I can't."

"Why not?" she demanded, lifting her arm to look at him.

"I haven't finished taking care of your ankle."

Faith gritted her teeth and tried to concentrate on something—anything—besides the feel of Cooper's strong hands stroking her arch, massaging the sole of her foot. "There's nothing to do," she said through gritted teeth.

"We need to put ice on it to keep the swelling down," he insisted, reaching into the white metal box.

Relieved that he'd stopped his sensual assault on her foot, she laughed. "And just where do you expect to find ice without a freezer or electricity to operate it?"

He grinned triumphantly and held up a small plastic bag. "Modern medicine is a wonderful thing."

Faith watched him grasp the bag in both hands and apply pressure in the middle with his thumbs. A slight pop followed, then he shifted it back and forth several times as if he was mixing the contents. When he placed the bag on her ankle, it was extremely cold.

"Chemical cold-packs are a staple of any well-stocked first-aid kit," he said, his smile so smug that she felt like punching him.

His hand still rested on her shin and she wasn't sure whether the shiver that ran up her spine was from the intense cold of the ice-pack, or the feel of his hand heating her skin just above it. Either way, she was beginning to understand the sensual combination of fire and ice.

Concentrating on the cold bag against her skin, she grimaced. "How long do I need to keep this on here?"

"About thirty minutes."

"My ankle will be frozen solid."

"No it won't." His low, sexy chuckle sent her temperature up another notch. To her relief he gave her shin a gentle squeeze, then closed the box and set it on the floor. Rising to his feet, he reached for the pillow beside her, folded it in half and propped her foot on top of it. "If you need me—"

"I'll let you know."

She wished he'd take his disturbing presence into the other room and let her regain at least a scrap of her common sense. With the exception of her injured ankle, she was extremely warm and getting warmer with each passing second.

Nodding, he started for the door, but turned back. "How do you like your coffee?"

"With cream," she said automatically.

He grinned. "Will powdered creamer do?"

"That will be fine. But you don't have to—"

"Yes, I do," he said, his expression turning serious. His gaze drifted to the floor and he ran his hand across the back of his neck. When he raised his head to look at her, the remorse in his eyes startled her. "I'm really sorry you got hurt, Faith. It's my fault and I intend to make it up to you."

She opened her mouth to tell him that it wasn't necessary, but he didn't give her the chance. He simply turned and left the room, ending any further discussion of the matter.

How could she tell Cooper, without making the situation even more embarrassing, that she hadn't been running from him, but from herself? How could she explain that she'd wanted to be held by a man again, to once again feel as if she were desirable? Even if it was just for a few moments.

She shook her head. She couldn't. There were some things that were better left alone. And explanations about her recent past and the reasons for her panic when he'd kissed her were among them.

When he returned holding a package of breakfast muffins in one hand and two coffee mugs in the other, he grinned. "I know it's not the healthiest of breakfasts, but it's about all we have."

"It's fine." Sitting up, she leaned back against the headboard and took one of the mugs from him. "Thank you." Faith took a sip of coffee and made a face. "You…weren't kidding when you said you make your coffee strong."

Cooper grinned. "Instant daylight." His expression turned hopeful. "I tried to tone it down a little by putting in an extra scoop of creamer. I hope it helped."

"Thank you. I can only imagine what it would taste like without it," she said dryly. She took another sip from the cup, then added, "But if you don't mind, I'll make the coffee tomorrow morning."

He opened the package of muffins, then held it out to her. "We'll see how you're getting around first."

"I'll be fine," she said firmly. She selected one of the delicious-looking blueberry muffins. "I'd be even better if you'd remove that ice-pack. My ankle is freezing. How much longer before we take it off?"

He laughed. "You're as impatient as Ryan and Danny."

"And they are?"

"My nephews." He checked his watch. "I'll wrap your ankle with an elastic bandage after you finish eating."

"How old are your nephews?" she asked, noticing a deep fondness reflected in his voice.

"Ryan's eight, he's Flint's son from his first marriage, and Danny's three. But don't tell them that." Chuckling, he shook his head and reached for the first-aid kit. "They think they're grown and ready to conquer the world."

Faith's chest tightened. She'd always wanted to have a son one day. But like so many of her other dreams, it just wasn't meant to be.

She finished the last of the muffin. Delicious before, it suddenly tasted like sawdust. "They sound like typical little boys," she said, her chest tightening at what she would miss.

"Oh yeah." He grinned as he removed a beige roll from the metal box. "My sister is never sure what she'll find in their jeans pockets when she puts them to bed at night. One time she found a small frog in one of Danny's pockets and another time she reached into Ryan's pocket and pulled out a garter snake.''

''Oh dear heavens!'' Faith shuddered at the thought of what that must have felt like. ''I'll bet that was a shock.''

''It just about sent Jenna into orbit. And believe me, she's not the type to scare easy.'' The rich sound of his laughter sent a shiver up Faith's spine. He had the sexiest laugh. ''Jenna screamed so loud that her husband, Flint, damned near broke his neck trying to get upstairs and the guys down at the bunkhouse grabbed their shotguns and came running to see what was wrong.''

Faith nodded. ''I'd have done the same thing.''

Cooper grinned. ''For a long time after that Jenna made Flint go through the boys' pockets before they came in from playing outside.'' He laughed and shook his head. ''But that doesn't stop us—them— from sneaking in a critter or two from time to time.''

''Us?'' She smiled. She could tell he was very close to his family and instinctively knew that he loved children. ''It sounds to me like their uncle might have helped them get some of those forbidden pets into the house.''

''Me?''

''Yes, you,'' she said, laughing.

''Well, I might have helped run interference when they found Peewee.''

''And what is Peewee?''

''A box turtle.'' He removed the cold plastic bag from her ankle, then lifted her leg from the pillow to rest it on his knee. ''They kept him hidden in a shoe box in the closet until I could get to town to buy an aquarium.'' He turned his head to look at her and grinning, admitted, ''By the time Jenna discovered that they had Peewee, we already had everything set up.''

He placed the rolled bandage to her foot and began wrapping her ankle. The warmth from his hand as he touched her chilled skin raised goose bumps along her arms.

''You sound like you're just as much of a boy as they are,'' she said. She cursed the breathless tone of her voice. She had to keep her mind off his disturbing touch. It was the only way she would manage to keep her sanity for the next several days.

''Yeah, in a lot of ways, I guess I am a big kid.'' His mouth turned up in a smile so sexy, Faith barely resisted the urge to fan herself. All she could think about was how wonderful those firm male lips had felt on her own.

Searching for something to keep her mind off the heat streaking through her body, she asked, ''Do you get to see them often?''

''I'm with the boys every chance I get.'' He finished wrapping the elastic bandage around her ankle, then attached the metal clamps to hold it in place. ''Now that I'm going to be living around here, I'll get to see them even more, which is fine with me. I love little kids.''

''It shows.''

Cooper placed her foot back on the pillow and closed the first-aid kit. He'd liked touching her, feeling her smooth skin beneath his callused palms. He wondered if the rest of her felt the same.

Damn! Thinking along those lines could spell disaster. If he intended to keep even a scrap of what little sense he had left, he'd better keep his distance.

He tried to think of something to say that wouldn't send his imagination into overdrive. "How about you? Do you have any nieces or nephews?" he asked, deciding that should be a nice safe topic.

She took a sip of her coffee. "I used to, but I lost my aunt status when the divorce was final."

Cooper barely managed to keep his mouth from dropping open. He couldn't believe any man in his right mind would let a woman like Faith get away. "How long were you married?"

She glanced down at her hands, then back at him. "We were together for four years."

He noticed the sadness in her eyes and wondered what had happened. Did she still love the man?

Cooper couldn't tell. But he'd bet every dime he had that the break-up of the marriage hadn't been her idea. The thought of someone hurting Faith in any way caused a burning in Cooper's gut that had him wishing for five minutes alone with the jerk. By the time Cooper was finished with him, the guy would wish he'd never been born.

"What happened?" he asked when curiosity got the better of him.

"I guess we just grew apart," she said, shrugging one shoulder. Her expression turned guarded. "He ended up going his way and I went mine."

Cooper could tell there was a lot more to the story than Faith was telling. But, he reminded himself, it was her story to tell and none of his business. If she wanted him to know more, she'd have explained further.

"What about a brother or sister?" he asked, trying to find a more pleasant subject—one that would erase the shadows in her pretty brown eyes. "Maybe one day they'll make you an aunt again."

"I was an only child," she said, smiling sadly. "I would have liked having a brother or sister, but shortly after I was born, my parents decided that family life wasn't for either one of them." She shrugged. "They divorced and went their separate ways. I was raised by my maternal grandmother."

"I'm sorry, I didn't mean to pry," he said, rising to his feet. If he didn't get out of there, and damned quick, he'd end up reaching for her, offering her comfort and…more. "I'll be in the kitchen. If I can coax a little water out of Old Faithful I'm going to peel some potatoes and use some canned beef to make a pot of stew. If you need anything—"

"I'll let you know," she said, handing him her coffee mug.

Her fingers brushed his and a jolt of electricity ran straight up his arm, then made a beeline to the region below his belt buckle. He swallowed around the cotton coating his throat. He had to get out of there before he did something really stupid like lying down beside her, taking her into his arms and kissing her until…

Without a word, he turned and walked straight to the kitchen. Setting the package of muffins, coffee mugs and first-aid kit on the counter, he opened the back door and walked out into the chilling rain. It was the closest thing he could find to a cold shower.

Armed with a broom, dustpan and garbage bag, Faith limped into the bedroom where the ceiling had fallen the night before. Cooper had brought her lunch, then saying something about checking out the barn, disappeared outside. And that was just fine with her. The more she was around him, the more she was reminded of how it felt to be wrapped in his strong arms, how his firm lips pressed to her own made her yearn for more.

She took a deep breath and shook her head to dislodge that train of thought. The reason she was up moving around in the first place was so she could get her mind off Cooper Adams. The more she found out about him, the more she liked him. And that was dangerous. She'd learned the hard way that where men were concerned, her judgment was extremely faulty.

But what woman wouldn't like a man like Cooper? He was kind and considerate. He loved children, placed a great deal of importance on family and didn't take himself too seriously. And he was, without a doubt, the sexiest man she'd ever encountered.

"What do you think you're doing?"

She jumped at the harsh sound of Cooper's voice. She'd been so lost in thought that she'd failed to hear him enter the house.

Turning, Faith found him standing in the doorway. Pushing the brim of his cowboy hat back, he planted his fists on his lean hips. Her heart pounded and her breath caught. The man was absolutely gorgeous and she wasn't certain if her accelerated pulse was due to being startled or because of his presence.

"I was hired to clean," she finally managed to say. She plucked the largest pieces of plaster from the bed to drop into the garbage bag. "And that's what I'm doing."

"I'll take care of this mess," he insisted, stepping

forward to take the bag from her. "You need to stay off that foot."

"We both know that it's only a mild sprain and nothing that requires bed rest." She gathered the four corners of the sheet and prepared to lift it off the bed.

"That's too heavy for you," he said quickly dropping the garbage bag to take the bundle of dust and plaster from her. "While I dump this outside, why don't you finish stripping the bed?"

"Deal." She started to stick her hand out for him to shake, but thought better of it. All things considered, touching him in any way probably wouldn't be wise. Instead she asked, "Do you think you could get some water out of Old Faithful? I'd like to wash these sheets this afternoon."

"Sure thing. I found some rope in the barn that I'll string up in the living room," he said helpfully. "You'll be able to drape them over it so they'll dry."

"Thank you. That should work perfectly."

She waited until he carried the sheet out of the room, then forced her mind back to the chore of removing the rest of the linens from the bed. That done, she took the broom, and began to sweep up some of the dust covering the floor. She leaned down to pick up a piece of plaster by the foot of the bed and froze. Just inches from her hand sat a small brown mouse, his beady eyes staring hungrily at her fingers. Her panicked cry was instantaneous and completely involuntary. If there was any creature she feared more than a spider, it was a mouse.

Cooper had just finished shaking the last of the dust from the sheet and opened the back door to enter the house when Faith's scream sent a chill up his spine and caused the hair on the back of his neck to stand straight up. His heart pounding against his ribs like a jackhammer gone berserk, he ran toward the bedroom where he'd left her.

Had more of the ceiling fallen? Possibly on her? Or could he have misjudged the seriousness of her injury and she was in extreme pain?

He skidded to a halt just inside the bedroom, his eyes widening at the sight before him. There stood Faith in the middle of the bed, the broom held more like a weapon than a household tool.

"What happened?"

She pointed a shaky finger at the floor. "Please get rid of it."

"What?" he asked, looking around. He didn't see anything. Had she seen another horny toad, or maybe a field spider?

"Mouse," she said, shuddering visibly.

If he'd been certain she wouldn't reach out and whack him with the broom she held, he'd have laughed out loud. But he was pretty sure Faith wouldn't see the humor in the situation. At least not at the moment.

"It's probably long gone," he said, continuing to scan the floor for the furry little critter. "You know, he's more afraid of you than you are of him."

"Not likely," she said with an unladylike snort.

Moving around the room, Cooper glanced up from his search. "He was just trying to find a nice cozy home for the winter. He didn't mean any—"

"Don't you dare say it," she warned.

"Why?"

"Because if you do I'll be sorely tempted to smack you with this broom."

Deciding it would be in his best interest to refrain from telling her that the little critter was harmless, Cooper continued to look for the mouse. Just when he was ready to give up, the tiny animal scampered out from under the bed and headed straight for his boot.

"Don't kill it," she said quickly.

"Okay." He threw the sheet he still held over it, then quickly squatted down to trap the mouse in the folds. "Any idea of what you want me to do with it now that I've caught the little guy?"

"Take it outside and turn it loose," she said, her voice sounding quite firm about the matter.

"What good will that do?" he asked, scooping up the mouse inside the sheet.

"He'll still be alive and I won't have to share the house with him," she said, sounding a bit more calm now that the mouse had been restrained.

Cooper couldn't help it. This time he threw back his head and laughed.

"What's so funny?" she asked indignantly. "There's nothing wrong with the catch-and-release method of dealing with mice."

"The damned thing will probably beat me back inside the house," he said as he rose to his feet and prepared to take it outside.

"There's a good chance he'll go somewhere else," she said, sounding hopeful. "Besides, I don't want it dead. I just don't want to occupy the same space with it."

Carrying the mouse several feet away from the house, Cooper released it, then watched it turn around and make a beeline straight back to the house. When it disappeared beneath the back porch, he shook his head and sighed heavily. He'd bet every dime he had that the furry little critter made its presence known again and ended up causing him more than a little grief in the bargain.

Five

"**Y**ou know, I can really sympathize with the pioneer women who helped settle this country," Faith said, draping the last sheet over the rope clothesline that Cooper had strung across the living room.

Along with the rope he'd found in the barn, he had discovered a washboard and washtub. It wasn't the most efficient way to launder clothes, but she'd be the first to admit that it was effective. The sheets were once again a nice, pristine white.

"Pioneers didn't have it easy, that's for sure," Cooper agreed from across the room. He'd been working on a window facing and from his muttered curses, it sounded like he could use some help.

When the board he held clattered to the floor for the second time, she walked over to where he stood. "I'm finished hanging the sheets. Is there something I can do to help?"

"I'd really appreciate it if you held this while I get the nail started," he answered, leaning down to pick up the board at his feet.

She watched him lift the window facing into place, then position it where he wanted. He'd rolled up the sleeves of his chambray shirt to just below the elbows and she found the flexing of his forearms absolutely fascinating. Never in her entire life had she seen anything quite so sexy.

"Faith?"

"What?"

"I asked if you're ready?" he repeated. Taking the nail from the leather pouch hanging from a belt around his waist, he gave her a curious look. "Are you all right?"

"Y-yes," she said, trying not to blush at being caught staring at his impressive sinew. She placed her hands where he indicated and to avoid the distraction of those muscles, made a point of looking down at her feet.

Out of the corner of her eye, she caught movement to her left and turning her head, watched a furry brown mouse head straight for her foot. When it raced over the toe of her shoe, then started climbing up the leg of her sweatpants, she couldn't help it, she let loose a startled cry.

Holding the nail with thumb and forefinger, Cooper had just drawn back to hit the nailhead with the hammer when Faith screeched like a cat with its tail caught in a door. His aim thrown off by her unexpected outburst, he missed the nail and brought the hammer down on the end of his thumb.

Normally, he did his best to watch the cuss words he used around a lady, saving the worst ones for when he was extremely frustrated, and always alone or with other guys. But the pain shooting through his thumb and up his arm loosened his tongue, and he couldn't have stopped the colorful string of words flowing from his mouth if his life depended on it. He dropped the hammer, cradled his hand to his chest and all but turned the air blue with creative phrases, while Faith danced around the room whooping and hollering like a sugared-up five-year-old trying to do a rain dance. Even with a sore ankle, she managed to put on an impressive display, and he stopped cursing to stare at her in complete awe.

"What the hell was that all about?" he demanded, when the pain in his rapidly discoloring thumb settled down to an aching throb.

She stopped prancing around and stood in the middle of the room, searching the floor as if she'd lost something. "A mouse...tried to crawl...up my leg."

It figured, he thought disgustedly. He'd known the minute he released that mouse and watched it cross the yard to run back to the house that it would end up causing him a butt-load of trouble.

He was extremely relieved to hear she'd been too preoccupied with getting rid of the mouse to notice his less than polite language. "I'd say after all that noise and the little jig you just danced, he's off somewhere having a mouse coronary about now," Cooper said dryly.

She shuddered, then looked at him for several long seconds before asking, "What happened to you?"

Apparently she'd noticed the way he held his hand protectively against his chest.

He shrugged one shoulder and held his thumb out for her inspection. The movement caused the throbbing to increase. He tried not to grimace from the pain, but failed miserably. "I missed the nail."

"Let me see," she said, rushing over to him. She took his hand in hers. "I caused you to hit your thumb, didn't I? I'm so sorry."

Her touch took his mind off some of the pain and he watched as she gently examined it. How could he tell her without making her feel worse that was exactly what had happened? He'd just as soon cut his tongue out first.

Shaking his head, he lied, "My aim was off. It would have happened anyway."

"Where's your first-aid kit?" she asked, her soft hands still holding his.

"I-in…" He cleared his suddenly dry throat. "In the kitchen. Why?"

"This should be iced down to prevent more swelling." Still holding his hand in hers, she led him into the kitchen. "Do you have another ice-pack?"

Nodding, he swallowed hard. At the moment, she could have led him toward a cliff and certain death, and he would have followed her without so much as batting an eye.

She urged him to bend his arm so that his hand was held high, then pointed toward the plywood table. "Sit down on that wooden crate and rest your elbow on the table. I want you to keep your thumb upright."

He started to tell her not to worry about it, that it had only been a glancing blow and that the throbbing had already started to ease down. Instead, he seated himself on the crate and dutifully elevated his hand.

Watching her prepare the ice bag, it suddenly occurred to him that he was seeing the "real" Faith—

calm, efficient and in complete control—for the first time since her arrival. As soon as she realized he'd been hurt, she'd collected herself and taken charge. He could also tell she loved every minute of it. But then, so did he.

"I can't tell you how sorry I am that I caused you to injure yourself, Cooper," she said, gently placing the bag over his thumb.

He barely managed to gulp back a groan. Her soft, warm hands holding his were enough to heat his blood, but hearing her velvety voice say his name sent it racing through his veins with the force of a record breaking flood.

"It's no big deal," he assured her.

"After having Percy in my class, you'd think I'd be over my aversion to mice," she said, sounding disgusted.

"You're a teacher?"

Nodding slowly, she sat down across the table from him. "I taught first grade."

"For how long?"

"Six years." She glanced down at her hands for a moment, then back at him. "When one of my students was getting ready to move to another state, he donated Percy to the class. Percy was a white mouse and really quite tame." She shuddered. "But he was still a mouse."

He wanted to ask her why she'd quit teaching— what had prompted her to leave her job and move to the Panhandle to seek employment as a housekeeper. But it was clear by the way she'd rushed on with her story about the mouse that she didn't want to go into it.

"And I'll bet that mice are right up there with

spiders on your list of creepy things you'd like to avoid," he said, grinning.

She looked relieved that he wasn't asking more questions about her change of career. "Absolutely," she said with a smile that damned near stole his breath.

He took the ice bag off his thumb and placed it on the plywood tabletop. He had to get away from her before he pulled her onto his lap and kissed her senseless. "I guess I know what I'll be doing while you fix supper."

A puzzled frown creased her forehead. "What's that?"

Rising to his feet, he grinned. "I'll be on a mouse safari."

"You won't—"

Cooper shook his head. "I won't hurt it. If I'm able to find him, I'll catch him and take him out to the barn where he can't terrorize you." He grinned. "Maybe with him out there my thumbs will be safe."

The next morning, Faith made sure to keep an eye on what was around her feet as she washed the few dishes they'd used for breakfast. Cooper had searched high and low yesterday before dinner, and later on during the evening, but hadn't found the mouse. He'd joked that it might have made the wise choice to move on and find another place to nest for the winter rather than risk taking part in another "mouse dance."

But Faith knew better. The little critter was prob-ably biding his time just waiting for another opportunity to run around and scare the living daylights out of her.

She dried the last of the dishes, placed them in the cupboard, then walked out onto the back porch. The sun had finally peeked out from behind the clouds this morning and she wanted to enjoy it while it lasted. With rain forecast for the rest of the week, there was no telling when it would appear again.

Noticing Cooper over by the barn, she walked down the steps and crossed the yard. "What are you working on now?"

"I'm trying to get this corral repaired before Flint brings cattle over here next week," he said, without looking up. "I'll need a couple of holding pens until I can get the pastures fenced."

He'd removed his shirt to work and Faith found herself thoroughly mesmerized by his shoulders and upper arms. Her ex-husband Eric had belonged to a gym for over ten years and hadn't come close to the muscle definition that Cooper had.

She waited for the sadness and regret to tighten her chest, as it always did when she thought of her ex-husband. But to her surprise, the feeling never came.

Maybe her grandmother had been right. Maybe moving away from the constant reminder of her shattered dreams was helping her to release the past and get on with building another life for herself.

Cooper turned to face her and the sight of his bare chest and rippling stomach struck her momentarily speechless. Cooper Adams was a hunk from the top of his wide-brimmed cowboy hat to the soles of his big boots. Glancing down at the worn leather, she fleetingly wondered if the old saying about the size of a man's feet and another part of his anatomy held true for Cooper. If so…

Good heavens! Had she taken leave of her senses?

"Was there something you needed?" he asked, looking about as sexy as any man possibly could.

She gulped. It wasn't so much a matter of what she needed as much as it was what she wanted. She *needed* him to put his shirt back on before she did what she *wanted* and reached out to touch his gorgeous body.

"Uh…no," she finally managed to say. "I just thought I'd enjoy the sunshine for a few minutes."

Pushing the brim of his hat back, he glanced up at the sky. "That's probably a good idea. I don't think it'll last more than another couple of hours." He pointed to a bank of clouds slowly building on the horizon. "It's my guess the next storm front will hit just before lunch."

"Will you be able to finish this before it starts raining?" she asked, trying not to stare at all that delicious looking masculine skin.

He raised his arms over his head to stretch. "Probably not. But I intend to get as much done as I can."

Faith stepped over to one of the fence posts and made a show of examining the aged wood. It wasn't that she was interested in the type of post it was or what condition it was in. She had no idea what she was looking at, nor did she care. But she had to get her mind off Cooper and the disturbing thoughts that were invading her obviously addled brain.

When he'd stretched, his muscles had flexed in the most fascinating ways and the action had drawn attention to his lean flanks and the fact that his snug jeans rode low on his narrow hips. It also revealed a thin line of dark brown hair just below his navel that disappeared beneath his waistband. She suddenly felt warm all over. And that wasn't good.

Shaking her head to dispel the image, she concentrated on what he'd said. He needed to get as much of the corral repaired as he could before it started to rain. Since she was his only source of help, there didn't seem to be any other choice.

She took a deep breath. She'd just have to ignore the fact that he had a body to die for.

"What can I do to help?" she asked, turning back to face him.

Cooper picked up the hammer and thought about the last time Faith had offered assistance. It was probably just his imagination, but he'd swear a tiny twinge of pain ran through his sore thumb.

He glanced at the northwestern horizon, then back at the corral. Damn! The clouds were building faster than he'd anticipated and the rain would be moving in within an hour or less.

"You don't mind?" he asked. "This isn't even close to the housekeeping you were expecting to do."

She grinned. "Oh, don't worry. I expect to be well compensated for the extra work."

Even though he hadn't hired her, technically as owner of the Triple Bar, Cooper was responsible for paying her wages. He didn't quite know how to tell her, but he wasn't exactly flush with cash. Oh, he had enough to get the ranch up and running, and he'd be able to get by easy enough until it started paying off. But it sounded like she was expecting a lot more than was usual for a housekeeper's wages.

"Exactly what did Whiskers promise you in the way of a salary?" he asked cautiously.

She named an amount that was about average for taking care of the cooking and household chores. "But Mr. Penn will be paying me dearly for the extra work I do around here." She grinned and he noticed the mischief twinkling in her luminous brown eyes. "One whisker at a time."

Cooper threw back his head and laughed. "Tell you what I'll do. I'll supply the tweezers and hold him down for you."

"You've got yourself a deal, cowboy," she said, giving him a smile that damned near knocked his socks off. "Now tell me what to do so we can get this fence up before it starts raining."

He picked up one end of a fence rail. "Do you think you can hold this while I nail it to the post?"

There was no denying it. He felt a definite twinge in his thumb that time. He ignored it. The mouse was somewhere inside the house and his thumbs should be safe. At least he hoped they would be.

"I'll do my best," she said, stepping forward to support the board he'd positioned on the post.

Thirty minutes and five fence posts later, Cooper pounded the last nail into place, then straightened from his bent position. "Thanks."

"I'm glad I could do something useful," she said, sounding as if she meant it.

"This would have taken me twice as long without your help," he said, wincing as he stretched out his sore muscles.

"What's wrong?" she asked, sounding genuinely concerned.

He rubbed the scar on his left side. "One too many wild bulls."

"I remember you mentioned that you rode bulls."

He nodded. "Until about five years ago. That's when I met up with two-thousand pounds of pissed off beef called The Shredder." He chuckled. "By the time he got finished with me, there wasn't a doubt in my mind why he'd been given that name."

"Was he the reason you have that scar on your back?" she asked, walking over to where he stood.

The concern in her voice, the look of compassion in her eyes, damned near knocked the breath out of him. But when she stepped behind him and started massaging his back, he lost the ability to breathe at all as her fingers gently worked at the knotted muscle just below his left shoulder blade.

She'd asked him something, but for the life of him he couldn't remember what it was. "What did you say?"

"I asked if that was the reason you have this scar on your back," she said patiently.

She traced his blemished flesh with her fingertips and he had to clear his throat before he could manage to get his vocal chords to work. "Uh, yeah, after tangling with him I decided I'd tempted fate enough."

"It looks like it was pretty serious," she said, her hands burning a trail everywhere they touched. "How long were you hospitalized."

"Uh, almost two weeks," he answered. He had to find something—anything—to take his mind off the way her talented little hands were making his body respond. Trying to remember the intense pain he'd suffered, he said, "I lost my spleen…and my heart stopped twice before they got me into surgery."

"My God, Cooper." Her hands stilled. "It sounds like you're lucky to be alive."

He gritted his teeth and tried to ignore his rapidly changing body. "That's what I'm told."

She flattened her hands on his shoulders and trailed them down to the small of his back. "I'd have to agree. You're very lucky," she said softly.

His body tightened and he had to force himself to take a breath. The kind of "lucky" he'd like to be would probably get him a good smack across the face.

Thankful she couldn't read his mind, he tried valiantly to hold himself in check. And he might have, had it not been for the feel of Faith's soft lips brushing against the blemished flesh just below his shoulder blade. But the moment she kissed his scar, a spark ignited in his gut and the heat quickly spread to his groin. He was hard as hell and wanted her with a fierceness that damned near knocked him to his knees.

Spinning around to face her, he placed his hands on her shoulders. "Faith?"

"Cooper, please…" Her guileless brown eyes reflected the same heat that had him hard as hell and wanting to throw caution to the wind.

"This isn't smart, Faith," he said, trying desperately to talk sense into both of them.

"I know," she agreed, sounding as short of breath as he felt. "Nothing can come of it."

She couldn't have put it more plainly if she'd drawn him a picture. Faith wasn't interested in a dust-covered cowboy with nothing but a run-down ranch and a pocketful of dreams.

A pang of disappointment knifed through him. But instead of turning her loose and walking away as far as his legs could take him, he pushed his hat back, then brought his hands up to tangle in her thick auburn hair.

"What the hell. I never was the brightest bulb in the lamp," he muttered, drawing her forward to lightly brush his mouth over hers.

Her lips were soft and receptive, and he couldn't have stopped himself from deepening the kiss any more than he could stop water from rushing over Niagara Falls. Her sigh of acceptance encouraged him and Cooper parted her lips to slip his tongue inside.

When he felt her hands tentatively come to rest at his waist, he reached down to take them in his own and bring them up to his shoulders. Wrapping his arms around her, he pulled her forward and held her to him as he once again tasted and explored her sweet mouth.

Faith knew she was playing a fool's game—that her assessment of men had proven too flawed in the past for her to ever trust it again. Unfortunately, with Cooper she couldn't seem to stop herself. She'd only meant to be helpful when she massaged the knotted muscles in his back, only wanted to help him relieve the pain of the old injury. But the temptation of his warm flesh against her palms had quickly built a fire inside her that was too strong to deny.

His arms drew her closer and the feel of his hard arousal pressed to her stomach made her knees weak and caused her disturbing introspection to dissipate.

Bringing her arms up to circle his neck, she told herself it was only for support, to keep herself from falling in a heap at his feet. But the truth was she wanted to be close to him, wanted to once again feel feminine and desired.

He lifted the tail of her shirt and skimmed his hand up her ribs to the swell of her breast. His callused palm cupping her, his thumb teasing her hardened nipple sent ribbons of desire swirling through every cell in her body. When had he unhooked her bra?

She didn't know and didn't care. His tongue stroking hers, his hands caressing her sensitive breast with such mastery, felt absolutely wonderful. Never in their four-year marriage could she remember the same degree of pleasure from Eric's touch that she experienced from Cooper's.

When he lifted his head to nibble kisses along her jaw to her ear, she moaned. "This is insane."

"You got that right," he said, his warm breath sending a shiver coursing through her.

"We can't—this can't go any farther." She wasn't sure if she was trying to convince herself or Cooper.

"It won't," he said, resting his forehead on hers. "I told you when you first arrived that you had nothing to fear from me." He took a deep breath, refastened her bra and took his hand from beneath her shirt. "And as much as I'd like to deny it right now, I'm a man of my word. Nothing is going to happen that you don't want happening, Faith."

She started to tell him that he wasn't the one she didn't trust, that it was her lack of judgment that scared her witless, but the words died in her throat.

A truck was slowly easing its way down the bumpy lane that led to the ranch.

And for the life of her, she couldn't figure out why she felt nothing but sadness at the thought that they now had a way off the ranch.

Six

"**I**s that your brother-in-law?"

Cooper glanced over his shoulder to see what had distracted Faith. He mentally cursed a blue streak as he watched a silver truck navigate its way around the many potholes in the dirt road leading to the house.

"No," he said, releasing her.

At any other time, Cooper would have been more than happy to have Brant Wakefield show up. Not only would the man pitch in and help finish the repairs on the corral, he was one of the best friends Cooper ever had. Hell, if not for Brant's skills as a rodeo bullfighter, Cooper would be pushing up daisies in some graveyard instead of standing there holding the most desirable woman he'd ever known.

But Brant's arrival represented a way for Faith to leave the ranch—to leave Cooper. And although having a way off the ranch was exactly what he'd wanted two days ago, it was the very last thing Cooper wanted now.

"Who is it?" she asked.

"Brant Wakefield." Turning to face the approaching truck, Cooper made it a point to stand in front of her while she straightened her shirt. "He's an old friend of mine."

"Well, whoever he is, I'm darned glad to see him," she said, stepping to Cooper's side.

"Me, too," he lied. He reached over to smooth her silky auburn hair where he'd run his fingers through it.

"Should I go inside and find a mirror?" she asked as she tried to finger-comb it into place.

He smiled. "You look beautiful."

"No, I mean—"

"You look just fine," he assured her.

He wasn't about to tell her that her perfect lips were swollen from his kisses or that her cheeks still wore the blush of passion. That would send her running into the house for sure. And, although it was none of the man's business what went on between himself and Faith, Cooper did want Brant to know she was off limits.

"Coop, you old dog, how have you been?" Brant called as he slowly got out of his truck.

"Looks like I've been doing better than you, Wakefield," Cooper said, pointing to the brace on his friend's knee. "What was the name of the bull and whose butt did you end up saving?"

Grinning, Brant limped over to where Cooper and Faith stood. "You think you know it all don't you, Adams?"

"Am I wrong?" Cooper asked, returning the man's good-natured grin.

"Nope." Sighing, Brant reached down and rubbed his knee. "I had another run-in with Kamikaze."

Cooper whistled low. "He's one of the worst for trying to hook a cowboy when he's down."

"You got that right," Brant said, nodding. Turning his attention on Faith, he asked, "And who is this lovely lady?"

Without thinking, Cooper slipped his arm around her waist, then making the introductions, added, "Brant and I go way back. He was the bullfighter who kept The Shredder from finishing me off once he had me down."

"It's nice to meet you, Mr. Wakefield." She shook his friend's hand. "Now, if you'll excuse me, I'll let you two gentlemen catch up on old times while I go inside and make sandwiches for lunch. You will be staying, won't you, Mr. Wakefield?"

"Sure thing, Ms. Broderick." The grin Brant sent Faith's way had Cooper grinding his teeth. "And call me Brant."

"Only if you call me Faith," she said, turning toward the house.

As she walked away, Cooper swallowed hard. He'd be damned if the woman didn't have the sexiest walk he'd ever seen. If given the chance, he could watch the sway of her sexy little hips all day long and never get tired of seeing it.

"Nice view, isn't it?" Brant asked from his shoulder.

"Best I've ever seen," Cooper answered without thinking. He could have cut out his own tongue. He might want Brant to steer clear of Faith, but he could do without the man's good-natured ribbing.

"So how long have you two been together?"

"She's my housekeeper."

He watched his friend survey the sagging porch and the plastic covering most of the windows and roof. "Sure. Whatever you say, Coop." Brant leaned one shoulder against the fence. "Then you wouldn't mind if I—"

"Leave her alone, Wakefield," Cooper warned. Turning, he yanked his shirt off the top rail of the corral and shoved his arms into the sleeves. "You've got more than enough women to keep you occupied. You don't need to add another."

When he looked up, Cooper cringed at his friend's ear-to-ear grin. "You're a damned liar and we both know it," Brant said, laughing. "You've got a case of the hot and bothereds for the lady that just won't quit. So you might as well 'fess up."

Jamming the tail of his shirt into the waistband of his jeans, Cooper shook his head. "You irritate the hell out of me sometimes, Wakefield."

Brant threw back his head and laughed. "That's what Morgan and Colt keep saying."

"They're right, too," Cooper said, grinning. Maybe if he got Brant to talking about his family, he'd drop the line of questioning about Faith. "How are those ornery brothers of yours?"

Brant shrugged. "Same as ever. Morgan's still trying to find out who inherited old Tug Shackley's ranch so he can buy them out and expand the Lonetree to the west. And Colt's joined the Professional Bull Riders."

"I thought he was riding broncs," Cooper said, gathering his hammer and sack of nails.

"That didn't work out." Brant shrugged one shoulder. "He said he didn't get the same rush out of riding horses that he did from riding bulls."

Cooper nodded. "I felt the same way when I was riding." He watched Brant rub at the brace on his leg. "You never did answer my question. Whose butt did you save from Kamikaze?"

His friend's easy grin disappeared immediately. "My dumb brother's."

"Colt?"

Brant nodded. "Most guys have the sense to turn out when they draw that black-heart beast," he said, referring to a cowboy's decision to let the bull out of the bucking chute without making the ride. "But not Colt."

"I understand how he felt about a turn out. I've only done it a couple of times myself." Cooper shook his head. "It's not easy paying your entry fee, then standing by to watch the gate swing open without you on the bull's back."

"I agree. But with some bulls it's a matter of survival." Brant stared off into the distance. "I'm just glad I was in the arena that day."

"You got a busted up knee out of the deal. What did Colt get?"

"He walked away without a scratch," Brant said, grinning.

Cooper wasn't surprised. Brant was one of the best bullfighters he'd ever seen.

"The sandwiches are ready if you two would like to come inside and have lunch," Faith said, stepping out onto the porch.

"We'll be right there," Cooper called as he and Brant started toward the house. Glancing up at the sky, he noticed that the bank of clouds he'd been watching earlier had changed directions and gone due south. "By the way, what do you have planned for the rest of the day, Wakefield?"

"Far as I know, I don't have anything going," Brant said with a shrug.

Grinning, Cooper slapped his friend on the back. "You do now."

Faith watched the two men finish the last of the sandwiches she'd made. "I guess that answers my question," she said dryly.

Cooper wiped his mouth with a paper napkin. "What's that?"

"Whether or not you two like peanut butter and jelly sandwiches," she said, smiling.

Both men laughed. "In the early days, when we both started out on the rodeo circuit, we lived off peanut butter and jelly sandwiches," Cooper said.

"Don't forget the times when we'd get a little money ahead and could afford baloney and cheese," Brant added.

Cooper grinned. "Or when we'd scrape up enough change from the floorboard of your truck to get a burger at one of the fast-food joints."

Brant chuckled. "Yeah, it felt like we were dining at a five-star restaurant."

Faith enjoyed listening to the men talk about their days together on the rodeo circuit. But she couldn't seem to stop herself from comparing the two.

Physically, they were both tall, handsome beyond words, and had physiques that could cause women to stop dead in their tracks to stare. Both were easy-going and friendly and had blue eyes. But that was where the similarities seemed to end.

Although Cooper had dark blond hair, while Brant's was black, that wasn't what Faith found so different about the two men. It was her reaction to them that had her baffled. When she'd shaken Brant's hand when he first arrived, she'd experienced none of the warm tingling sensations that she did with Cooper. All Cooper had to do was walk into a room and her heart would start to flutter. And when she looked into his gorgeous blue eyes, she felt as if she might drown.

Heat flowed through her and she decided it would be in her best interest to concentrate on something besides Cooper and the way he affected her.

"Did you ever ride bulls, Brant?" she asked, careful to avoid Cooper's warm gaze.

"Good lord, no!" He looked shocked. "I've got more sense than that. I've always been a bullfighter."

"I thought that was a Mexican or Spanish sport." She rose from the table to clear away their plates. "I didn't realize they had it in rodeo, too."

Cooper shook his head. "It's not that kind of bull-fighting, darlin'. Brant puts himself in front of the bull to distract him while a cowboy dismounts and gets out of the way."

"That sounds dangerous," she said, hoping she didn't sound as breathless as she felt. Whenever Cooper called her "darlin'" in that sexy drawl of his, it seemed hard to take in air.

"It's not that bad," Brant said.

"Don't let him fool you," Cooper said, shaking his head. "There are dozens of cowboys who owe their lives to this man, including me. That's why you'll never hear a bullrider have anything but praise and gratitude for the job he does.''

"Aw, shucks, Coop. I never knew how much you cared," Brant said, grinning mischievously.

Laughing, Cooper stood up. "Don't let it go to your head, Wakefield. You've already got an ego the size of Texas and I'll be damned if I'm going to be responsible for making it bigger. I'm surprised you find a hat that fits now.''

"You're just jealous 'cause I get all the girls," Brant said, winking at Faith.

"Like that little blonde down in Tucson?" Cooper shot back.

Brant groaned. "You would have to remember that.''

"That's just the tip of the iceberg." Cooper opened the door and walked out onto the porch. "There was that time over in Albuquerque that you…''

Faith watched the two men file out the door, their good-natured jibes fading as they walked toward the corral. It was clear to see they were the best of friends and had been for a long time.

A lump formed in her throat and tears threatened. Until a year ago, she'd had a friend like that. Charlotte Turner and Faith had grown up next door to each other and they'd been as close as any sisters could ever be. She'd been able to trust Charlotte with everything.

Or so she'd thought.

But having her oldest and dearest friend use her deepest secret fear that she'd never be able to have a child against her had been almost more than Faith could bear. Charlotte had purposely become pregnant with Eric's baby because she knew how important having his own child was to him, and because she'd fallen in love with him.

Sniffling, Faith grabbed the broom and began to sweep the worn hardwood floor. Thinking about her best friend dredged up some of the best memories of her life, as well as the most painful.

But more than anything else, it proved that her judgment of people never had been reliable.

Thunder rumbled in the distance as Cooper folded his arms across his chest and proudly gazed at his newly repaired corral. With Brant's help, Cooper had replaced three fence posts, the rest of the missing rails and hung a new gate. By his calculations, they'd been able to accomplish in a few hours what it would have taken him and Faith at least a full day.

Cooper pulled his shirt on, then began collecting the tools they'd used. "Thanks for the help, Wakefield. I owe you one."

"Hey, man, I had the time and you needed the help," Brant said, grabbing his own shirt from the top of a post. He looked around. "By the way, what's the deal here? I thought you told me you'd bought a ranch that needed a little work. This place looks like it will take a month of Sundays to get into shape."

"One word," Cooper said sardonically.

Brant chuckled. "You don't have to tell me. It was Whiskers, wasn't it?"

By the time Cooper finished explaining the purchase arrangement for the property and about the scheme the old man had cooked up to strand Cooper and Faith together, Brant was laughing so hard he had to wipe the moisture from his eyes. "He sure is a crafty old buzzard."

"I was thinking more like a mean old goat," Cooper said, grinning. He spotted a roll of screen wire and an idea began to form. "I have one more project I need your help with before you leave."

"Besides taking you and Faith back to civilization?" Brant asked.

Cooper's stomach clenched into a tight knot. He'd purposely avoided thinking about them having a way off the ranch. But whether he wanted to or not, the subject had been broached and there was no turning back.

"Faith will probably take you up on the offer." He felt as if someone had punched him in the gut as soon as he said the words. Taking a deep breath, he added, "But I think I'll stay and see what I can get done around here before the cattle arrive."

Brant gave him a wicked grin. "That'll give me a good hour or more to get to know Faith on the way to Amarillo."

Cooper knew that he was being baited, but he couldn't stop himself. "I'm warning you—"

"I get the message, Adams." Brant laughed. "I just had to see how far gone you are."

"I'm not—"

"Save it," Brant said, holding up his hand. "I wasn't born yesterday. Even I'm smart enough to see that you're a goner." He smiled knowingly. "And unless I miss my guess, the lady has it just as bad for you."

"You've got it all wrong, Wakefield."

Brant folded his arms across his chest and stubbornly shook his head. "I don't think so. What do you want to bet she stays here with you when I take off?"

Cooper glared at the man. "Did that bull kick you in the head while he was tearing up your knee?"

"Nope." Brant's grin sorely tempted Cooper to reach out and strangle the man.

"Look around, Wakefield. What woman in her right mind would want a man with a run-down ranch and just enough money to get by?"

"A woman in love."

"Now I know that bull kicked you in the head," Cooper said disgustedly. "You just don't remember it."

His friend's answering laughter irritated the hell out of Cooper. "Just wait and see what happens when I take off tomorrow morning. If Faith doesn't stay here with you, I'll come back next week and help you fence every pasture this place has. And we both know how much I hate stretching barbed wire."

"You'll help anyway," Cooper said with confidence.

Brant grinned. "I know. But I had to have something to bargain with. Now what was that project you wanted me to help you with?"

"You're never going to believe this."

"Try me."

"We're going to build a cage for a mouse," Cooper said, tossing Brant the roll of screen wire.

"You're right," Brant said, shaking his head. "I don't believe you."

The next morning, Faith poured coffee for the two men to have with their muffins. "I'd like to thank both of you for building that cage and confining the mouse,'' she said, remembering how they had searched most of the evening before they finally found the annoying little animal. ''Maybe now I can get something done, instead of watching what's around my feet.''

''No, problem,'' Brant said, cheerfully. He devoured the banana-nut muffin and reached for another. ''Cooper said it tried to run up your leg the other day.''

She shuddered. ''I'm afraid I really put on a show that day, didn't I, Cooper?''

When he nodded, but didn't say anything, she wondered if she was making the right decision. He'd been strangely quiet all morning.

Deciding there was no better time than the present to find out, she cleared her throat. ''Cooper, I have something I need to ask you.''

He slowly set his coffee cup on the plywood tabletop. ''What do you need?''

You, a traitorous little voice in her muddled brain whispered. She wasn't sure where it had come from, but she fully intended to ignore it.

''If you don't have a problem with it, I'd like to stay until your brother-in-law brings the cattle.'' Rushing on before he got the wrong idea, she explained, ''I have a score to settle with Mr. Penn.''

She knew her excuse was as flimsy as tissue paper and that she'd lost every ounce of sense she possessed. But she'd lain awake half the night, thinking about leaving the Triple Bar Ranch—leaving Cooper—and she'd come to only one conclusion. She was going to stay with him. Then she'd tossed and turned the rest of the night, trying to rationalize her decision. Getting even with Mr. Penn was the only plausible excuse she'd been able to come up with.

Relief flowed through her when she watched a slow smile turn up Cooper's firm lips. "That would be fine with me, darlin'," he said. His sexy baritone sent shivers along every nerve in her body and she suddenly felt warm all over.

Brant's chuckle turned to a cough when boots shuffled under the table. "I won't be leaving until after lunch," he said, reaching down to rub his shin. "Let me know if you change your mind."

"I doubt that will happen," Cooper said, his gaze holding hers captive. "Faith deserves to take a strip off Whiskers's hide for what he's pulled."

She glanced away in time to see Brant look from her to Cooper, then grinning like the Cheshire cat, rise to his feet. "All righty then. It's settled. Come on, Coop. Let's get that junk cleaned out of the tack room before I take off."

Four hours later, Cooper and Faith stood on the porch waving as Brant pulled away from the house. Cooper liked having his best friend around most times, but this wasn't one of them. He was more than glad to see the backside of Brant's pickup truck as he drove away.

The way he saw it, he had three, maybe four days left with Faith before Flint and Whiskers arrived. He knew it was pure insanity, since nothing could ever come of the attraction between them. But he wanted to spend as much time with her as he could before she walked out of his life for good.

"Brant is very nice," she said congenially. "I'm

glad he was able to help you get the corral and barn ready for the cattle.''

"I can't think of anyone else I'd rather have in my corner when the chips are down," Cooper agreed. But he didn't want to talk about Brant, or corrals or cattle.

Taking her by the hand, he started down the porch steps. "Come on, darlin'. I have a surprise for you in the barn."

Faith gave him a grin that damned near knocked him flat. "It's not another one of your harmless critters, is it? Because if it is, I'd just as soon pass on the opportunity."

"Nope. This is something I think you're really going to like. Brant and I found it while we were cleaning out the tack room." When they reached the barn door, he covered her eyes with his hand. "Now keep in mind that it isn't perfect and probably not what you're used to. But it's better than what we have."

"So you're trying to tell me to keep an open mind?" she asked, laughing.

He chuckled. "Something like that." Leading her to the room in the middle of the barn, he took his hand from her eyes. "So what do you think?"

"Is that what I think it is?" she asked, her face breaking into a happy smile.

"Sure is." He rocked back on his heals. "It's an honest to goodness, antique bathtub. After I get it scrubbed up, I'll carry it up to the house so you can take a real bath instead of having to make do with a wash pan and a sponge."

Her reaction was everything he'd hoped it would

be. She threw her arms around his neck and planted a kiss on him that had him deciding to poke around the barn a little more and find other treasures that would make her happy.

Seven

Humming along with the classical music coming from the battery operated CD player she'd found buried in one of her suitcases, Faith lifted the last pot of hot water from the camp stove. She poured it into the old-fashioned bathtub, then added cool water to get the temperature just right. Sprinkling in a generous amount of the bath salts she'd brought with her, she inhaled deeply as the scent of roses filled the room. It smelled heavenly. She couldn't wait to immerse herself in the water and soak until it turned her completely pruny.

Gathering her long hair, she twisted the length of it, then used a large toothed clip to secure it to the back of her head. While the water had heated on the stove, she'd taken off her clothes, put on her fluffy pink terrycloth robe and collected everything she'd need. There was only one thing left to do before she lit the candles she'd arranged by the tub, stripped off her robe and slipped into the water. She needed to find some way to secure the back door to keep Cooper from accidentally walking in to find her lounging in the tub.

It wasn't that she didn't trust him to respect her privacy. She did. But he knew nothing about it. She hadn't decided to coax water from Old Faithful and indulge herself until after he'd gone outside. She was a bit bothered by the fact that she'd be bathing in one corner of the kitchen, but that's where the kerosene heater was and the other rooms were simply too chilly to even consider.

She took a deep breath and looked around. What could she use to secure the door? It didn't have a lock. When she'd first arrived, she'd found that odd and very disconcerting. But the more she thought about it, the more she decided that it probably hadn't been necessary for the occupants who had lived there so many years ago. The house was quite a distance from the main road and completely hidden from view. And neighbors certainly weren't a problem. Besides herself and Cooper, there wasn't another living soul for miles and miles.

In her search to find a way to block the door, she spotted several large packing cartons that they hadn't yet emptied. Perfect. They should be heavy enough to insure her privacy.

She lifted the towel she'd hung over the window in the door to make sure Cooper was still down by the barn. When a rusty bucket came sailing out of the big open door to land on the rapidly growing pile of things to be hauled away, she breathed a sigh of relief. He was too intent on getting the barn into shape to stop anytime soon.

Smiling, she turned and shoved the heavy boxes against the door, lit the candles and slipped off her robe. She stepped into the bathtub and sat down. It was short and narrow and she had to bend her knees a bit, but the water felt wonderful when she sponged it over her arms and upper chest. As she washed herself with the soft mesh puff, she decided it was quite possibly the most luxurious bath she'd ever taken. She smiled. Compared to washing off in a washpan like she'd had to do for the past few days, it felt positively lavish.

Resting against the high back of the tub, Faith allowed the soft scent of roses and the soothing music of Chopin to surround her. She closed her eyes in sheer pleasure. A trip to an expensive spa couldn't make her feel any more relaxed and pampered than she did at that very moment.

When the sound of thunder echoed across the land, Cooper tossed another piece of junk on the pile outside the barn door and looked up. The clouds had gathered while he'd been inside cleaning out the feed room and within the next few minutes the sky was going to open up and pour. Unless he wanted to dodge lightning bolts, he'd better knock off work and head for the house.

Dusting off his hands on the seat of his jeans, he glanced toward his new home. The place wasn't much right now. But it would be. He'd make sure of it. It already looked better, since he and Brant replaced the broken support post on the back porch. At least now he didn't have to duck his head when he reached the top step.

A sense of pride filled his chest, then spread throughout his body. For the first time in his life, he had a place of his own—a place that wasn't portable. Having been raised on the rodeo circuit, even as a child his home had been a camper on the back of a pickup truck. His family had traveled like nomads from one rodeo to another while his dad chased his dreams, first as a steer wrestler, then as a bullfighter.

But Cooper had finally made the decision to put down roots and it felt good. Damned good.

He just wished that Faith hadn't shown up to see the ranch the way it looked now. He'd have preferred her arrival a little later, after he'd made some much needed repairs and renovations. Maybe then…

Cooper shook his head. No sense worrying about that now. She'd just the same as told him she wanted no part of him or his run-down ranch. Besides, now was not a good time to be thinking about a wife. When he did find a woman to share his life, he'd have a ranch to be proud of and something more to offer her than a leaky roof and bathroom facilities that involved a fifty-yard sprint and a flashlight after dark.

His steps heavier than they'd been only moments ago, he walked to the house and up the porch steps. The sound of music caused him to stop short. Where had she come up with something to play music? He shook his head at his own foolishness. She'd probably unearthed it in one of her suitcases. He chuckled. He wouldn't be surprised at anything she found in Mt. Samsonite. Hell, as big as some of those pieces were, he wouldn't be surprised if a family of four could be housed quite comfortably in one of the damned things.

But as he listened to the classical music he shook his head again as he reached for the doorknob. She liked that lofty stuff, while he preferred the down to earth sound of country tunes. It was just one of many ways they were different, and additional proof that a woman like Faith could never be interested in a cowboy like him.

He twisted the knob, but stopped short when the door refused to budge. Glancing up, he grinned at the towel covering the window in the door. Women liked curtains, and it appeared that Faith had been busy using whatever she could find to fashion some.

But why had she locked him out of his house? Deciding that she probably wanted to surprise him with the little feminine touches she was making to his home, he tapped on the glass.

"Faith?"

Nothing.

The music from her CD player was pretty loud. She probably couldn't hear him.

Knocking on the wooden frame, he put a little more force behind his effort and managed to push the door open a couple of inches. A soft flowery scent drifted through the crack. "Faith, let me in," he called.

Still nothing.

What was going on? Could she have fallen while she was hanging things over the windows? Was she hurt?

His mind ran through a half dozen different scenarios—all of them ending with Faith injured and lying unconscious somewhere inside the house.

Placing his shoulder against the door, he shoved with everything he had and suddenly stumbled into the room amidst a pile of large boxes.

"Faith?" he shouted as he pushed himself to his feet.

Candlelight in the far corner of the kitchen drew his attention and he felt as if someone had punched him in the gut. There she sat in the old bathtub, naked as the day she was born, and looking more beautiful than any woman he'd ever had the privilege to lay eyes on.

She blinked owlishly in an obvious effort to get her bearings, and it was clear to see she'd fallen asleep while taking a bath. When her eyes focused on him, she let out a startled squeak and to his immense disappointment, quickly tried to cover herself. But the old tub was small and there was no way for her to sink lower into its depths.

"What are you doing in here?" she asked, her cheeks turning a very pretty rose color. "I thought you were clearing junk out of the barn."

He had to fight with everything he had to keep from grinning. She looked so danged cute sitting there with her silky auburn hair piled on top of her head, trying to hide her full breasts behind that puffy little bath thing.

The urge to smile died and his mouth felt as if he'd swallowed a mouth full of desert dust when he noticed how little the bath puff covered. Her coral nipples were drawn into tight buds and he couldn't have looked away if he'd wanted to. Which he didn't.

Fully clothed, Faith was beautiful. But nude, her satin skin glistening in the candlelight, she was a vision of everything a woman should be—soft, sensual and seductive beyond words.

Heat streaked through him and his lower body tightened predictably. "It…uh, started raining," he said, shoving his hands in his front pockets to relieve some of the pressure of his suddenly tight jeans.

He could tell she'd noticed his arousal, but instead of looking away, she seemed as fascinated by his body as he was by hers. He took a step forward.

A sudden flash of light illuminating the room, followed closely by a loud clap of thunder caused them both to jump and brought Cooper back to reality. What the hell did he think he was doing? He'd told her he could be trusted not to put the moves on her and he'd keep his word if it killed him. The way his lungs refused to take in air and his heart pounded against his ribs, he decided that it just might, too.

Turning around, he forced himself to take a deep breath as he headed toward the door. "I'll be out on the porch," he said through gritted teeth. "Once you've dressed, let me know and I'll empty the bathtub."

Faith waited until Cooper shoved the boxes out of the way and slammed the door behind him before she grabbed the towel beside the tub and stood up. What in heaven's name had gotten into her?

Her cheeks burned and she bit her lower lip to hold back an embarrassed sob as she vigorously rubbed the moisture from her skin. Heaven help her, but she'd wanted him to see her, wanted him to want her as badly as she wanted him. And if the bulge in his jeans and the hungry look in his eyes were any indication, he did.

Thank goodness the intrusive sound of the storm

had brought her back to her senses. But how was she ever going to face him again? Was she so desperate to be held, to once again feel desired, that she had practically issued Cooper an invitation to make love to her?

Quickly pulling on her extra baggy, blue sweatshirt and jeans, she mopped the floor where she'd splashed water out of the tub when she'd jerked to a sitting position. She blew out the candles and lit the lantern. The overcast sky outside had caused the room to be darker than usual and they would need the light in order to see. But the candles were too romantic, too intimate, too seductive.

Deciding she couldn't delay calling Cooper inside any longer, she opened the door. "You can come in now."

She didn't look at him as he crossed the room and began bailing water from the bathtub. She couldn't. Her mind was trying to sort through her tangled emotions. Humiliation still heated her cheeks at the way she'd shamelessly acted when he'd stood there staring at her. But it was the thrill she'd felt when she'd seen the hungry desire for her in his deep blue gaze that scared her senseless.

Once he'd hauled the last of her bath water outside, he walked over to Old Faithful and began working to coax water from the spout. "If you don't mind, I think I'll take a bath and shave while there's still light," he said.

Nodding, she turned to leave the room. "No problem. I'll stay in the living room until you're finished."

"You know, there's nothing to be embarrassed

about,'' he said, setting a large pot of water on the camp stove to heat.

Good grief! Was she that transparent?

Without looking at him, she shook her head. ''Please, let's just forget—''

He surprised her by wrapping his arms around her from behind and pulling her back against him. ''Darlin', I could live another hundred years and not forget the sight of your beautiful body,'' he said close to her ear.

His low, deeply impassioned statement sent a shiver up her spine and created a pang of longing in her chest that threatened to suffocate her. ''Cooper, I can't—''

''It's all right, darlin','' he said, holding her close. ''Like I've told you before, you can trust me. I give you my word that nothing is going to happen that you don't want happening.''

It wasn't that she didn't trust him. And it certainly wasn't that she didn't want him. She did. But she couldn't trust herself not to start longing for the things she knew she'd never have.

Stepping from his arms, she started to walk away.

''Faith?''

''I'll be in the living room,'' she said without turning to face him. ''Let me know when you've finished dressing and I'll start dinner.''

Cooper dried the plate Faith handed him and placed it in the cabinet. He hated the sadness shadowing her pretty brown eyes, hated the silence between them. She hadn't said more than a handful of words in the past two hours.

''Thanks for supper,'' he said, trying once more

to start a conversation. "There's not a whole lot of ways to fix Spam on a camp stove, but that was really good."

"You're welcome," she said, turning to wipe off the counter. "Would you mind emptying the dishpan for me?"

As he dumped the water outside he wondered how he could get them back to the easy companionship they'd shared for the past few days. He could tell she was no longer embarrassed by his walking in on her while she took her bath. But he couldn't understand the sadness that had taken its place. If anything, he'd have thought she'd be hopping mad that he'd barged in like a charging bull.

He shook his head. There were some things about women he just didn't understand and probably never would.

The rain dripped off the porch roof and he shook his head. If the weather would cooperate, he'd take her out and show her some of the things he'd found in the barn. Things that were sure to make her smile, like the hula girl lamp or the castle made out of hundreds of glued together bottle caps. But since the storm showed no signs of letting up, that was out of the question.

Opening the door, he reentered the kitchen deep in thought. What could he do to lift her spirits?

Looking around, his gaze landed on the CD player still sitting on a box in the corner and he felt a smile slowly lift the corners of his mouth. "Faith?" When she glanced up from the book she'd started reading, he asked, "Would you mind if I used your CD player?"

"Of course not." She got up from the plywood

table to remove the classical disk she'd been playing while she bathed. "Are you going to listen to it in here?"

"No. I think I'll take it into the living room," he said, reaching for the handle.

As he picked up the unit and headed toward the front of the house, he purposely didn't ask if she'd like to join him. He had a few things to take care of first.

Setting the player on a wooden crate, he pushed all of the packing cartons into one corner and took down the rope clothesline. Fortunately, the room was large and they would have plenty of room to move around.

By the time he finished, it was getting dark outside. "Where did you put the candles?" he asked as he walked back into the kitchen.

She glanced up from the book to give him a curious look. "On the counter by Old Faithful. Why?"

"It's getting dark outside and I need a little light to keep from stumbling over something and breaking my neck," he said, grinning.

"Would you like to use the lantern?" she offered.

The last thing he wanted was the brighter light. "No. You need it for reading."

Faith watched him collect all of the candles, then stroll back down the hall. Why on earth did he need so many?

As the sound of lively country music filtered in from the front of the house, she shrugged and turned her attention back to her book. The less she thought about Cooper Adams, the better off she'd be. But when she found herself reading the same page for the third time, she closed the book and abandoned any pretense of trying to read.

Her initial embarrassment at her reaction when he'd found her naked had given way to deep sadness. He wanted her and she wanted him. But if they made love, she couldn't trust herself not to fall head over heels for him. And, if the longing that held her tightly in its grip was any indication, she was already well on her way to doing just that.

Something deep inside told her that Cooper was exactly the man he appeared to be—honest, hardworking and loyal to a fault. But she'd trusted her instincts once before and been proven devastatingly wrong.

She'd misjudged her husband and best friend, and hadn't even suspected they were having an affair. The first that Faith knew of anything going on between them had been when Eric asked for a divorce to marry Charlotte because she was pregnant with his child.

"Faith, darlin', are you all right?" Cooper asked from her shoulder.

Looking up, she noticed the concern on his handsome face. She'd been so lost in her disturbing memories, she hadn't noticed that he'd walked back into the room.

"I'm fine."

"Are you sure?" he asked. "You looked like you were a million miles away."

"I think I was," she admitted, shaking off her dismal mood and forcing a smile.

"Are you back now?" he asked. He grinned and her heart skipped a beat.

"Absolutely," she said, feeling a little breathless.

How could she think about the past with Cooper standing so close?

"I'm glad. I have somewhere I want to take you for the evening," he said.

Lightning flashed and thunder rumbled. Where could he possibly take her with it raining cats and dogs outside?

Taking her by the hand, he pulled her to her feet. A warm tingling sensation immediately raced up her arm from the contact. "Would you do me the honor of joining me in the front of the house, ma'am?"

Laughing at his mischievous expression, she followed him down the hall. "What's this all about?" she asked, raising her voice to be heard above the music coming from the CD player.

When they came to the end of the hall, he moved his arm in a sweeping gesture and leaned down to whisper in her ear. "I'm taking you to the Triple Bar Dance Hall, ma'am."

Her eyes widened and she brought her hand up to cover her startled gasp. He'd lit every candle they had to cast a soft glow over the cleared room and draped a sheet over a packing carton for a table. Two small wooden crates had been arranged on either side of the table for seating and a single taper stuck in a longneck beer bottle served as the centerpiece.

Tears blurred her eyes and she had to blink several times in order to hold back the threatening flood of emotion. She'd never seen anything more romantic or touching in her entire life.

"Do you like it?" he asked, sounding hopeful.

She nodded and had to swallow around the lump in her throat before she could speak. "Cooper, this is the nicest thing anyone has ever done for me."

Raising up on tiptoes, she placed a kiss along his chiseled jaw. "Thank you."

Looking sexier than any man had a right to look, he touched the back of his hand to her cheek. "I'm glad you like it." He gazed down at her for endless seconds before his expression changed to a teasing grin. "It looks pretty crowded in here tonight, but I think I see a table over there," he said, pointing toward the box.

He obviously wanted to lighten the conversation, which was fine with her. "I believe you're right," she said, playing along.

They crossed the room and once he'd seated her, Cooper made a show of looking around. "The waitress must be taking a break. I guess I'll have to go up to the bar to get something for us to drink. What would you like?"

She pretended to think for a moment. "I'll have whatever you're having," she finally said.

Grinning, he tipped his hat. "I'll be right back."

In no time at all he was seating himself on the crate opposite her. He placed two juice boxes on the table, then stuck narrow straws in the tops. "I got myself a beer, but I thought you might like wine."

"Nice choice," she said, smiling back at him.

The song that had been playing ended and another one began.

"Would you like to dance?"

"I'm afraid I'm not very good at country dancing," she said, shaking her head.

He rose to his feet and took her hand. "Come on, it's easy. I'll teach you."

She stood up and followed him into the middle of

the room. "I have to warn you, I'll probably step all over your feet."

"That's going to be kind of hard to do, since we'll be doing the Stroll," he said, laughing.

"Stroll?"

Nodding, he draped his arm across her shoulders. "It's a Texas tradition." He instructed her where and how to hold his hands, then how to do the steps.

They'd made a full circle of the hardwood floor before she realized that she was actually doing the dance correctly. "This is fun and not nearly as hard as I thought it would be," she said, laughing.

He grinned as they started around the room another time. "I told you it was easy."

By the time the CD ended and the changer switched to another disk, Cooper had not only taught her the Stroll, he'd taught her the Two-Step and a couple of line dances as well.

"This is really fun," she said, breathlessly.

"Ready to take a break?" he asked, leading her over to the table.

She sank down onto the crate she'd used for a chair and took a sip from her juice box. "Cooper, do you mind if I ask you a question?"

"Shoot," he said, taking a long draw on his straw.

"Why do you wear your hat while you're dancing?" She paused. "In fact, I don't think I've seen you take it off more than once or twice since I've been here."

He shrugged. "No self-respecting Texan would be caught dead dancing the Two-Step or the Stroll without it," he said as if it were the most reasonable explanation in the world. "In fact, there are only a couple of things a Texan will do without wearing his hat.''

She could just imagine what one of them was. His sexy grin told her she was right.

''Have you ever tried not wearing your hat when you dance?'' she asked, hoping he didn't notice the heightened color she was sure tinted her cheeks.

''Nope.''

''Why not?''

He slowly set his juice box down and the grin he sent her way curled her toes. ''It's like Samson and his hair. With it, he's a hell of a man. Without it, he's nothing but a scrawny little wimp. Same thing holds true for a cowboy. With his hat on, he's a dancing fool. Take it off and he has two left feet.'' Grinning, he leaned over as if sharing a secret. ''Besides, it looks real good.''

She laughed and shook her head. ''That hat is your security, isn't it?''

''Something like that.''

When a slow song began he took her hand in his, then stood and pulled her to her feet. ''Ready to try a slow one?''

The scent of his clean, masculine skin, the feel of his warm palm pressed to hers, made the ability to speak impossible. Nodding, Faith willingly followed him onto their private dance floor.

He reached down to take her hands and place them on his wide shoulders. Then, positioning one of his thighs slightly between her legs, he wrapped his arms around her waist and drew her close.

Moving them around the floor, he gazed down at her and the edge of his hat brim rested on the top of her head. It seemed to lend an intimacy that took her breath.

Lightning illuminated the room and thunder crashed. She barely noticed.

"Cooper?"

"What?"

"What are we doing?" she asked, her tone nothing more than a throaty whisper.

"We're dancing," he said, his gaze never wavering from hers.

"No, I mean—"

He placed his index finger to her lips. "Just dancing, darlin'."

She tried concentrating more on the song and less on the man holding her to his hard body. Big mistake. The words were every bit as provocative as their dancing. Maybe more so.

Cooper's hands roamed the length of her back and every cell in her body tingled to life. Resting her head against his shoulder, she had to remind herself to breathe.

When he cupped her breast and teased the tight tip with his thumb, her knees threatened to buckle and she couldn't for the life of her seem to draw in air. His muscular thigh between hers and the friction it created as he guided them around the floor sent heat streaking through her veins to pool in the lower part of her stomach.

The weather outside seemed to be intensifying, but it was nothing compared to the storm raging within her own body when he cupped her bottom with his other hand and pulled her closer. He pressed his arousal against her stomach and nuzzled the sensitive skin of her neck. Sparkles of light flashed behind her closed eyes and her heart felt as if it turned a cart-wheel inside her chest.

As the song ended, she started to pull back. He held her tightly to him.

"Just let me hold you a little while longer, dar-lin'," he said, his tone husky.

It was pure insanity on her part, but that was exactly what she wanted him to do. "Cooper?"

"Whenever you tell me to let you go, I promise that I will," he said, brushing his lips against hers.

His mouth settled over hers and anything even resembling a thought escaped her. She was too caught up in the warmth of his kiss, the teasing of his tongue as he parted her lips and slipped inside to stroke her own.

The longing she'd fought from the moment she'd met him welled up inside her and created an aching need that only Cooper could cure. She wanted him more than she'd ever wanted any man in her entire life.

"Faith?"

Pulling back, she stared up at him for endless seconds before conceding defeat to the desire that she'd felt from the moment she'd first seen him. The way he'd said her name, the hunger in his deep blue eyes told her more than words that he wanted exactly what she wanted.

He'd told her there were very few reasons why a cowboy removed his hat. She was absolutely certain she knew what one of them was.

She took a deep breath and smiled. "Cooper, take off your hat."

Eight

Cooper's heart slammed against his ribs, then took off in overdrive at Faith's request that he take off his hat. "Are you sure?" he asked. The last thing he wanted was for her to have regrets tomorrow morning.

She reached up and removed his Resistol. "The only regret I'll have is if we don't make love," she said softly.

He searched her face for any indication that she had even a shadow of a doubt about making love with him. When he found none, he pulled her against him and buried his face in her silky auburn hair. He'd bet good money that Faith didn't trust easily. But the confidence in him that he'd seen in her luminous brown eyes had damned near brought him to his knees. He'd make this the most memorable night of her life, or die trying.

Releasing her, he walked over to the CD player and changed disks. When the classical music that she'd been playing while taking a bath filled the room, he blew out all but one of the candles, then took her by the hand.

He used the remaining candle to light their way as they silently walked into the bedroom and, setting it on a box in the corner, took her into his arms. Her body fit against him perfectly and lowering his mouth to hers, he let her know without words how much her trust meant to him.

Her lips clung to his a moment before she opened for him to deepen the kiss, and her eagerness excited him more than anything he could have ever imagined. She was letting him know that she wanted him as much as he wanted her, that she was as caught up in the magic as he was.

When he slipped his tongue inside to explore and tease, she whimpered, then wrapped her arms around his neck to thread her fingers in the hair at the nape of his neck. Her warm touch, the sound of her desire and the sweet passion he tasted as she tentatively met his invasion, sent his blood pressure soaring and caused his lower body to throb with need. He'd never in his life been this turned on by a single kiss.

Shifting to relieve the pressure of his suddenly too tight jeans, he reached down to cup her bottom and lift her into the cradle of his hips. He wanted her to know what she did to him, wanted her to realize the power she held over him.

He brought his hands up to the tail of her sweatshirt and sliding his palms along her ribs, cupped her full breasts. "You aren't wearing a bra," he said,

feeling her already tight nipples bead even further
against his palms.

She slowly shook her head. "I was in such a hurry
to get dressed, I...forgot."

"I'm glad." He gently circled his thumbs over the
tight nubs.

She closed her eyes and he felt a tiny tremor
course through her. "Mmmm."

"Feel good?"

"Y-yes."

"It's going to feel even better," he promised,
reaching down to pull her shirt over her head.

She lifted her arms to help him and once the garment lay on the floor at their feet, he sucked in a
sharp breath. He'd caught a glimpse of her breasts
that afternoon when she'd tried to hide behind that
puffy little bath sponge. But it was nothing compared
to the unrestricted view he now enjoyed.

Supporting the weight of them with his hands, he
lowered his mouth to first one puckered coral bud,
then the other. "So soft. So sweet." He raised his
head. "You're beautiful."

"So are you," she said, sounding breathless.

Raising his head, he smiled. "Guys are too flat
and angular to be beautiful."

"You are." The sincere expression on her pretty
face just about knocked his size thirteen boots right
off his feet. "Please take your shirt off, Cooper."

He couldn't have denied her if he'd wanted to.
Which he didn't.

Tugging his shirt from his jeans, he grasped the
tails and pulled the chambray open with one quick
jerk. He'd never been more appreciative of snap clo-
sures on a shirt than he was at that very moment.

When she placed her soft, warm hands on his chest, heat shot straight to his groin and his heart thumped so hard that he wouldn't have been surprised if it cracked a couple of ribs. As she ran her palms over the rise of his pectoral muscles, her fingers tracing his own puckered nipples, Cooper took deep breaths and tried to slow down his libido. But when she explored the ridges of his stomach, her fingers dipping slightly below the waistband of his jeans, he stopped breathing altogether.

Groaning, he took her hands in his and shook his head. "If you keep that up, you're going to give me a heart attack."

"I like touching you," she said. Her smile sent his temperature up another ten degrees.

"And I like touching you, darlin'," he said, bending down to take off her shoes and socks. He caught her gaze with his and held it as he unsnapped her jeans and pulled them and her panties over the flare of her hips and down her slender legs.

Careful to keep his attention on taking off the rest of his clothes, he didn't allow himself the pleasure of looking at her until after he'd pulled off his boots and socks, then shucked his jeans and briefs. He knew the limit of his control. He also knew he'd just about reached it.

Straightening to his full height, he tossed his clothes on top of Faith's and turned to face her. The air in his lungs stalled and his mouth went bone-dry. Candlelight painted her satiny skin with a soft glow and highlighted her firm, uptilted breasts, trim waist and the curve of her gently rounded hips.

Lightning flashed and thunder boomed, but they barely noticed.

At the sight of Cooper's powerful body illuminated by the streak of light from the storm, Faith's breath caught and her pulse pounded in her ears as loudly as the thunder crashing outside. His wide shoulders and sculptured chest tapered down to narrow hips and lean flanks. Her gaze skipped lower and she swallowed hard. Proud and strong, his manhood rose from a mat of dark brown curls. He certainly validated the old adage about the size of a man's feet being an indication of the size of his other parts.

Her gaze flew to his and he must have sensed her hesitation. "Don't worry, darlin'," he said, stepping forward to take her into his arms. Nuzzling her neck, he whispered close to her ear, "We'll fit together just fine."

The feel of skin against skin, male hardness pressed to female softness, sent electric currents of pure desire sizzling along every nerve in her body. "It's been quite a while," she admitted, wondering if that throaty voice could really be hers.

Placing his index finger beneath her chin, he tilted her head up to meet his dark blue eyes. "You trust me, don't you, Faith?"

"Yes."

His reassuring smile made her feel as if she'd melt into a puddle at his feet. "We're going to take this slow and easy and I'm going to love you in every way a man can love a woman."

Her stomach did a back flip and a shiver of anticipation slithered up her spine at his candor. But before she could tell him that was exactly what she wanted, he lowered his mouth to hers. His tongue slipped between her lips and set off a hot, dizzying current of pure electrified desire flowing to her most secret places. All thought ceased as she reveled in the man holding her to his strong body.

Breaking the caress, Cooper trailed moist kisses down the slope of her breast, then took her tight nipple into his warm mouth. Ribbons of tingling need wove their way around her and formed a tight coil in her lower stomach. Her knees trembled and she had to clutch his arms to keep from falling.

"Easy, darlin'," he said, raising his head to look at her.

The heated passion she saw in his eyes, the promise of complete fulfillment and his request for her trust, released something deep inside of her and at that moment she knew for certain that she'd fallen hopelessly in love with him.

"Cooper, please—"

Apparently he understood her unspoken plea because he led her over to the bed. "I need to get some protection," he said, turning back to the pile of clothes on the floor.

"It's not necessary," she said, quietly.

He hesitated. "You're protected?"

A deep sadness swept through her as she nodded. She couldn't bear to tell him there was no need for any type of prevention, that she was unable to have children.

Taking her into his arms, he lowered her to the bed and stretched out beside her. He gathered her to him, and gazing down at her, tenderly covered her lips with his. His callused palm smoothed over her skin with such infinite care, it brought tears to her eyes and she forgot all about prevention or her inability to become pregnant. He erased all that with his touch, his mind-numbing kiss.

He slid his hand down her side to caress her hip, her inner thigh making her quiver with need. But when he cupped the curls at the apex of her thighs, his finger dipping into the soft, moist folds to stroke and tease, spirals of sheer ecstasy swirled through her. The feelings he drew from her were so intense that she gripped the sheet beneath her and arched into his touch.

"Feel good, darlin'?" he asked, raising his head to look down at her.

When he entered her with his finger to test her readiness for him, the coil in her belly tightened and turned into a sweet ache. She squeezed her eyes shut and fought for sanity as waves of sensation flowed through her.

"Cooper, please—"

In answer to her broken plea, he spread her thighs with his knee and levered himself over her. She felt the tip of his strong arousal probe her and she tensed in anticipation of his invasion.

"Open your eyes, Faith." When she did as he commanded, he held her gaze with his. "Just relax. We're going to take this slow and easy."

The blaze of need in his dark blue eyes took her breath. But she could tell he was holding himself in check, making sure that she was as ready for their lovemaking as he was.

"Trust me to take care of you?" he asked.

She nodded without hesitation. At that moment, she trusted him more than she'd ever trusted anyone.

Slowly, gently, he pressed forward with such care she thought she'd die from the ecstasy of it. When he had filled her completely she felt him quiver inside of her as he held himself in check. Her heart swelled with love as she realized Cooper's sacrifice.

He remained perfectly still, and she instinctively knew he was giving her time to adjust to him, to the exquisite stretching of her body by his. He was placing her above his own needs. He was taking care of her.

Cupping his face with her hands, she smiled up at him. "Love me, Cooper."

A groan rumbled up from deep in his chest and he shuddered against her. "Darlin', it will be my pleasure." He pulled his hips back, then eased forward. "And I give you my word it'll be yours, too."

His rhythmic thrusts created an inner storm in Faith that rivaled the weather outside and she wrapped her arms around him to keep from being lost. The heat spiraling through her burned higher and brighter, tightening the feminine coil until it clouded her mind to anything but the love she felt for him.

A flash of lightning momentarily lit the room and seemed to charge the atmosphere with urgent anticipation. Time stood still as Cooper's body built the tempest to a crescendo and she wasn't sure if the sound in her ears was the thunder outside or the pounding of her own heart. As she gave herself up to the whirlwind of her climax, the hot tide of passion washed over her as wave upon wave of fulfillment surged through her soul.

Moments later, she heard Cooper groan deeply, then shudder as spasms overtook him and he released his essence deep within her. When he collapsed on top of her, Faith tightened her arms around him, reveling in the differences between his body and hers, anchoring him to her as his own storm subsided.

His breathing eased and he levered himself up on his elbows. "Are you all right?" he asked, brushing a strand of hair from her cheek.

"I feel incredible." She closed her eyes and stretched. "That was the most beautiful experience of my life."

"Mine, too." He rolled to his side and gathered her to him. "The next time—"

"There's going to be a next time?" she asked, her body tingling to life at the promise in his blue gaze.

"Oh, yeah."

"And when would that be?"

He chuckled. "Just as soon as I recover, darlin'."

"And how long do you think that will take, Mr. Adams?"

He brushed her lips with his. "In about five seconds, Ms. Broderick."

Wrapping her arms around his neck, she waited a few moments, then grinning, informed him, "Time's up, cowboy."

Cooper rolled over to put his arm around Faith, but he met empty air. He opened his eyes to see where she was, but the bright shaft of sunlight streaming through the windows quickly had him squeezing them shut. Cursing, he threw back the covers, sat up and swung his legs over the side of the bed.

"Burning daylight is not the way to get things done around here," he muttered as he reached for his clothes.

He stopped suddenly and listened to the country

music drifting in from the other part of the house. He didn't even try to stop the satisfied grin he was sure split his face from ear-to-ear. Faith was playing one of the CDs they'd danced to the night before— the one he'd played just before they'd made love.

The memory of their lovemaking, of her supple body taking him in, draining him of every ounce of energy he possessed, sent heat coursing through him. They had come together several times during the night and still he burned for her. He shook his head. How was he going to get any work done around the ranch when all he wanted to do was take Faith in his arms and love her until they both dropped from exhaustion?

He shook his head. He had a feeling he could make love to her for the rest of his life and still never get enough of her, never satisfy the need she created in him.

Taking a deep breath he abandoned that train of thought. He had nothing to offer her but the promise he'd one day make a success of the ranch. And that wasn't enough. A woman like Faith deserved a whole lot more than he could give her.

But he refused to dwell on that. They had until Flint and Whiskers showed up and that's what Cooper intended to concentrate on.

Lost in thoughts of all the ways he planned to love her during the few short days they had left together, he stopped short at the sound of male voices coming from the kitchen. Damn! Flint and Whiskers had arrived earlier than they were supposed to. And although that's exactly what Cooper had wanted four days ago, it was the last thing he wanted now.

Taking a deep breath, he slowly walked into the

kitchen to find his brother-in-law and Whiskers sitting at the plywood table having coffee with Faith. He wanted nothing more than to draw back and punch the hell out of both of them. When they left to go back to the Rocking M later in the day, they'd be taking Faith with them, taking her away from him.

"Would you like a cup of coffee, Cooper?" Faith asked when she glanced up to see him standing in the doorway. The glint of panic he detected in her expressive eyes ripped right through him.

"Thanks," he said, nodding. He dragged a crate from the corner and sat down. When she placed a mug on the table in front of him, he smiled. "By the way, I just finished putting up that rod in your bedroom closet," he said, hoping she'd catch on.

What went on between the two of them when they were alone was nobody's business but their own. He didn't give a damn about himself or what others thought of him. But he was determined to protect Faith, and if that meant telling lies the size of Texas, he'd gladly do it.

Looking relieved that he'd fabricated a plausible explanation for his not being present to greet Whiskers and Flint, she smiled. "Thanks. Now I can hang up some of my things."

"Whiskers, don't you have something to say to Cooper and Faith?" Flint spoke up, his expression determined.

The old man cleared his throat. "Well, I reckon as how I don't have a whole lot of choice."

"Whiskers," Flint warned.

"Tarnation, Flint, let me do this my own way," Whiskers grumbled. Turning to Faith, he said, "I'm mighty sorry for strandin' you here with Coop. I don't know what got into me. It was a mean thing to do and I shouldna done it.''

Cooper watched Whiskers hang his head for effect and almost burst out laughing. He'd seen Whiskers in action before and knew beyond a shadow of doubt that the old man didn't mean a word of what he'd just said. It was Cooper's guess that once his sister, Jenna, had gotten wind of the incident, she'd threatened to turn the old man's room at the Rocking M ranch house into a playroom for the boys if he didn't apologize. And since Whiskers thought the sun rose and set on Jenna, Cooper knew the old guy would walk barefoot across hot coals if that's what it took to get back in her good graces. He also noticed that the apology hadn't included him.

"No, you shouldn't have done that to either of us, Mr. Penn,'' Faith agreed. "But what's done is done.'' She patted Whiskers's arm reassuringly. "We'll just forget about it as long as you promise not to do anything like that again.''

Whiskers's head popped up so fast, Cooper thought he might have wrenched his neck. "You got my word, Miss Faith,'' he said, giving her a toothless grin.

Cooper and Flint both coughed at the same time to cover their laughter. It was the biggest load of bull they'd ever heard the old geezer dish out.

"Where are Jenna and the boys?'' Cooper asked, once he'd recovered.

"At home,'' Flint said, rising to his feet. "The boys caught colds while we were at Disneyworld and Jenna's got some kind of stomach flu. She thought the way the weather's been with all the rain it would be best if they stayed home.''

"Damn. I really wanted Faith to meet Jenna," Cooper said without thinking.

As soon as the words left his lips, Cooper could have bitten his tongue in two. Flint and Whiskers both knew how close Cooper was to his sister, and that it was extremely significant that he wanted her to meet Faith.

"We'd better get those cattle unloaded and in the corral," he said, to cover his blunder. He stood up and reached for his hat, but it wasn't on the peg where he always hung it before he went to bed at night.

"Where's your hat, Coop?" Whiskers asked, his eyes twinkling merrily.

"I think you left it in the living room last night," Faith said, starting down the hall. "I'll get it for you."

As soon as she left the room, Whiskers chuckled. "Only one reason I know of that would keep a man from hanging his hat on the peg before he goes to bed at night."

Cooper gave both men a hard stare. "I was tired."

Laughing, Whiskers patted Cooper's shoulder as he passed by him to go outside. "Yeah, and I'm still a young buck with piss and vinegar runnin' through my veins."

"Come on, Whiskers," Flint said, grinning. "Let's get started unloading the trailer before you get both of us into trouble."

The door had barely closed behind them when Faith walked back into the room. "Thank you," she said, handing Cooper his hat. "I appreciate the excuse you gave them for not being around when they arrived."

"How long had they been here before I got up?"
he asked, jamming his hat onto his head.

"About five minutes," she said, looking relieved.

Reaching for her, he pulled her to him. "How do
you feel this morning, darlin'?"

She wrapped her arms around his waist and laid
her head against his shoulder. "Absolutely wonderful."

"I'm glad." He kissed the top of her head. "I feel
pretty damned good myself."

"Cooper?"

"What, darlin'?"

Faith hesitated. In the past few days, he hadn't
mentioned anything about her staying with him after
Whiskers and Flint brought the cattle. And she really
couldn't think of one good reason to remain on the
Triple Bar, other than she didn't want to leave him.

Sighing, she decided there was no good way to
broach the subject, nor was she willing to run the
risk of having him say no if she asked him if he
wanted her to stay. "You'd better get out there and
help them with the cattle before they come looking
for you," she finally said.

"There's really nothing for you to do here in the
house," he said, leaning back to give her a look that
all but melted her bones. "Why don't you come outside and see what's going to pay the bills around here
one day?"

"Sure," she said, heartened that he wanted her to
see a part of what he was working to build.

When they walked out into the yard, she saw a
long stock trailer filled with red, white-faced cattle
hooked to the bed of an extended cab pickup truck.
It was backed up to the corral that Cooper and Brant

had repaired, while another truck with a shorter trailer connected to it was parked close by.

"Coop, where you want me to tie the horses?" Whiskers called.

"I've got a couple of stalls ready in the barn," Cooper answered. Faith watched him help Flint lower the tailgate on the longer trailer. "Put them in there."

As Whiskers led two beautiful reddish brown horses into the barn, a stream of about a dozen cows and calves trotted out of the trailer and into the enclosure. Standing by the fence, Faith was fascinated by Cooper's efficiency. It was easy to see he'd worked around livestock all his life.

"You're going to have trouble with that one," she heard Flint say as he nodded toward a calf standing by itself on the far side of the corral.

"Why's that?" Cooper asked, closing the gate. He rested his forearms on the top of the fence and gazed at the calf Flint had indicated.

"Her momma got stuck in the mud down by the creek last night and by the time my men found her this morning, it was too late." Flint walked to the cab of his truck and removed a bucket with a long nipple attached to the side and a large bag of some kind of animal food. Handing it to Cooper, he added, "They've been trying to get her to feed, but haven't had much luck."

"It was that heifer that dropped her calf out of season," Cooper answered.

Faith wasn't sure how he could tell which cow was missing. To her they all looked alike. But that didn't matter. As an idea began to take shape, she stepped up to where the two men stood. "What will you have to do to take care of her?" she asked.

"I'll have to mix up calf formula and feed her once every few hours." Cooper shook his head. "Damn. I don't have time to be raising a bucket baby right now."

She bit her lower lip as she gathered her courage. She knew that she'd have to leave in the near future, but not yet.

Trying not to sound as if his answer would mean the world to her, she asked, "Would it help if I stayed around for a while longer and took care of the calf for you?"

Nine

Sucking in a sharp breath, Cooper's pulse took off at a gallop. Faith had a way to escape the primitive conditions they'd been forced to live in the past few days, but she was willing to stay?

"Are you sure you want to do that?" he asked, hoping with all his heart that was exactly what she wanted. "It's going to demand a lot of your time."

She smiled. "My dance card's pretty crowded, but I think I can make room for one little red calf."

Her reference to dancing sent a fair amount of adrenaline surging through his veins. She was letting him know that she was staying, not because she wanted to care for an orphaned calf, but because she wanted to be with him. He felt like picking her up, taking her inside the house and making love to her for the rest of the day.

"Darlin', you've got yourself a job." Grinning, he

handed her the feed bucket. "Welcome to mother-hood."

For a split second, he could have sworn that a deep sadness clouded her eyes, but it was gone as quickly as it appeared. "I think I'll name her Penelope," she said, turning to stare at the little calf.

He frowned. "Penelope?"

"Don't you like it?" she asked, her expression hopeful.

"It's not that I don't like it. It's fine." He shrugged. "But normally a rancher doesn't name his cattle."

"That doesn't matter," she said, smiling. "Penelope's special. She's named after my grandmother." She laughed and the sound was like music to his ears. "They both have the same color hair."

Her enthusiasm and sweet smile had him deciding that she could name every animal he owned if she wanted to and he'd readily go along with it. "Then Penelope it is," he said, smiling back.

"How old is she?"

"She was born about five weeks ago," he answered.

Turning on him, her stormy expression surprised him. "She's only a month old and she's still in there with all those big cows? No wonder she's standing there shivering. She's just a baby and scared to death. Go get her."

It appeared Faith was taking this mothering thing pretty seriously. "Where am I going to put her until I get another stall in the barn ready?"

"I don't care, but she's not staying in there."

Whiskers walked up and slapped Cooper on the

back, his toothless grin wide. "While I was puttin'
the horses up, I nosed around—"

"Why doesn't that surprise me?" Cooper asked
dryly.

Snorting, the old man raised his chin a notch and
finished, "You could put her in the tack room."

Cooper looked over at Flint for help. But the smirk
on his brother-in-law's face and his noncommittal
shrug made Cooper want to punch him.

Resigned, he opened the gate and motioned for
Flint to follow him. "You take the left side and I'll
take the right."

In no time, they had the calf cornered and gathering her into his arms, Cooper carried Penelope out
of the corral.

"Will she be all right in the tack room by herself?" Faith asked, sounding genuinely concerned.
She reached out and gently ran her hand along the
calf's red hide.

Cooper stared at her a moment as he watched her
soothe the frightened animal he held. Faith would be
a wonderful mother some day. He only wished he
could be the father of her babies.

A pang of deep longing tightened his chest. He'd
always planned on having a wife and kids one day,
and she was just the type of woman he'd always
wanted. But the timing was lousy. There was way
too much to do to this place, too many repairs to be
made.

His steps heavier than they'd been only moments
before, he walked toward the barn. He couldn't ask
Faith to saddle herself with a man who had nothing
to offer her but hard work and a truckload of prom-

ises. She deserved better than that. A hell of a lot better.

Settling Penelope in the tack room, he went back outside and found Flint and Whiskers preparing to climb into the cab of Flint's truck. "I appreciate your bringing the cattle and horses." Giving Whiskers a pointed look, Cooper added, "And for returning my truck."

"You don't have to thank me." The old geezer had the audacity to give Cooper a toothless grin as he added, "I been thinkin' it all worked out right fine."

Cooper knew Whiskers wasn't referring to returning the truck as much as he was about taking it in the first place.

"If you get tired of the primitive conditions, you're both more than welcome to stay at the Rocking M," Flint offered.

Cooper glanced at Faith to check for her reaction to the offer, but an almost imperceptible shake of her head quickly had him grinning and shaking his own head. "Thanks, but I don't want to waste thirty minutes just driving over here. It's time I could be getting something done." He held up the new cell phone battery Flint had handed him earlier. "Besides, now that I can make calls, I'll be able to get the power company out here to hook up the electricity as soon as I get the house rewired."

Flint nodded as he got into the truck. "If you change your mind, you know where we are."

"Did you mention Sunday dinner, like Jenna said?" Whiskers asked, getting in on the passenger side.

Flint snapped his fingers. "Damn, I almost forgot.

Jenna said to tell you to be over at our place by noon Sunday.''

Cooper grinned. ''We'll be there. Tell the boys I'll take them on another critter hunt if they're over their colds by then.''

''I'll tell them,'' Flint said, his grin wide. ''But I've got better sense than to tell Jenna.'' Starting the engine, he and Whiskers waved as they drove away.

Draping his arm around Faith's shoulders, Cooper waited until the truck disappeared from sight before he pulled her into his arms. ''I'm glad you decided to stay,'' he said, brushing his mouth over hers.

She smiled as she wrapped her arms around his waist. ''Penelope needs me.''

He smiled down at her. ''Is the calf the only reason you decided to stay?''

''No.''

''What's the other reason?''

''I haven't finished my work for the day.''

''Work?''

Nodding, she stepped from his arms and started walking toward the barn. ''After I take care of feeding Penelope I have to—'' She stopped to glance at him over her shoulder, and giving him a smile that sent his blood pressure out of sight, finished, ''Make the bed.''

Faith stirred the warm water into the powdered calf formula, then tested it on her arm to see if it was too hot. Confident that the milk was just right, she eyed the gallon bucket with the nipple on the side. It wasn't full, but it still looked like an awfully large amount for one little calf.

"Cooper, are you sure this isn't too much?" she called down the wide barn aisle.

Poking his head around the side of the stall he was cleaning, he shrugged. "Flint said they were having trouble getting her to eat, but if she starts nursing like she's supposed to, it'll be about right." He walked toward her. "I almost forgot to tell you, you'll have to be careful to brace the bucket when you start to feed her. You won't be able to just hold it by the bail."

"Why?"

He grinned. "Because she'll butt her head against the bucket just like she would against her momma's udder and you'll wind up with calf formula all over you."

"Ouch," Faith said, wincing. She could just imagine how a poor mother cow would feel. "Why do calves do that?"

"It helps get the cow's milk started," he explained. He lifted the bucket. "Come on, I'll show you how to hold it to keep her from knocking it out of your hands."

He carried the bucket down to the tack room where he'd confined Penelope, then showed Faith how to hold the bucket to steady it. "She's still a little skittish about people," he said, walking slowly over to the corner where the little calf stood shivering nervously.

Faith heard him murmur soothing words as he caught the calf and guided her to where Faith stood holding the pail of milk. "Come on, sweetheart," she said, adding her encouragement.

She watched Cooper kneel down and take hold of the nipple. He squirted a little milk toward Penelope and as soon as it landed on her nose, the calf ran her tongue out to lick it off.

"That's it, little one." He squirted more milk onto the calf's nose. "You're hungry, aren't you?" Grinning, he looked up at Faith. "Once she gets the taste and figures out where it came from, she should hit that bucket like a defensive tackle trying to break through the line."

It took several squirts for Penelope to realize where the milk came from, but when she did, she took the nipple into her mouth and butted the pail so hard Faith almost dropped it. "You were right about her butting against it," she said, laughing. "Will she drink all of this at one time?"

"Probably." He stood up and scratched Penelope's red back while she noisily sucked on the nippled bucket. "If the cow was around, she'd nurse whenever she wanted. But now that you're her momma, she'll have to get used to a schedule."

Faith's chest tightened when he referred to her as Penelope's mother. He had no way of knowing how long she'd wanted to be a mother, how she and Eric had tried to have a baby for over a year with no luck. She stared down at her bovine charge and blinked back tears before Cooper noticed. At least she'd get to mother something, even if the baby in question had a long tail that wiggled every time she ate.

"If you two will be all right, I'll go finish getting her stall ready," Cooper said.

"We'll be fine." Faith watched the level of milk in the bucket descend as Penelope butted against it and sucked noisily on the nipple. "Is there a lot left to do?"

He shook his head. "I just need to put down a fresh bed of straw."

"Where did the straw come from?" She hadn't seen Flint or Whiskers unload anything but the horses and cattle.

"Whiskers wasn't joking when he said he'd thought of everything." Cooper chuckled. "There's about twenty bales of straw stacked in one of the other stalls and about two weeks supply of horse and cattle feed stored in the feed room." He walked to the door. "When Penelope gets finished eating let me know and I'll carry her down to her new home."

Faith watched him go, then looked down at the calf he had coaxed into eating. Cooper was the most gentle, caring person she'd ever known. The patience he'd shown as he worked to help Penelope learn to find nourishment from the bucket had amazed her. And if she had any doubts about her feelings for him, they'd just been erased.

She was completely and hopelessly in love with Cooper Adams.

Faith bit her lower lip to stop its nervous trembling. She knew nothing could ever come of a relationship with Cooper. He deserved to have a family and she refused to deprive him of it. But she had a few more days to store up a lifetime of memories. And that was exactly what she intended to do.

She just hoped when the time came for her to leave that she was able to go without leaving her entire soul behind.

Cooper had just finished spreading straw over the dirt floor of the stall when he felt something tickle the back of his neck. Reaching up, he brushed his hand across his nape. When he felt the tickling again, he turned to find Faith standing behind him holding a straw in her hand.

He grinned. "Oh, so you want to play, huh?"

"How do you know that was me?" she asked innocently as she started backing away from him. "It might have been a spider that spun his way down from one of the rafters, tickled your neck, then climbed back up."

"Was it?"

Laughing, she took another step backward. "No, but it could have been."

When she turned to run from the stall, he caught her around the waist and pulled her to him. "Have you ever seen a tickling spider, darlin'?"

"No."

"Then I guess I'll have to show you one," he said, running his fingers over her ribs.

She giggled and squirmed to break free of his grasp. "Cooper—"

"What?"

"Stop…tickling me."

Her wiggling threw them both off balance, and making sure he held her so that he took the brunt of the fall, they landed in the soft bed of straw. With her sprawled across his chest, their legs tangled together, his body responded with a speed that made him dizzy. In a matter of seconds he was fully erect, his veins pulsing with need.

She must have noticed the change in his body because she stopped laughing to stare down at him. He watched as the teasing light in her eyes faded and a hunger that matched his own began to replace it.

"Faith?"

She stared down at him for several long seconds, then giving him a slow, sexy smile that damned near caused him to have a heart attack, she said, ''Your hat came off when we fell.''

He hadn't even noticed. Seeing it lying a few feet away, he smiled back at her. ''So it did.''

She ran her finger down his nose, then traced his lips. ''Should I get it for you?'' Her finger dipped into his mouth. ''Or do you want to leave it where it is for a while?''

His grin faded and he sucked in so much air, he thought his lungs might explode as he caught on to her meaning. Was she really asking him if he wanted to make love here in the barn?

He needed to make sure he wasn't reading things wrong. ''Well...'' He had to stop and clear his throat in order to make his vocal chords work. ''What do you think, darlin'?''

She appeared to give the matter some thought, then leaning down, whispered in his ear, ''I think you'd be more comfortable with your hat off, Cooper.''

The sound of his name on her velvet voice, the look of hunger in her pretty brown eyes and the feel of her soft body draped over his, sent a shaft of deep need straight to his groin. At that moment, he didn't care if he ever wore his hat again.

Cupping her cheeks with his hands, he drew her head down to his and pressed his mouth to hers. Her softness created a warmth in his chest that spread throughout his body and he moved to deepen the kiss. But Faith had other ideas.

When she slipped her tongue inside to stroke and tease his, the heat ignited into a flame that threatened to consume him. She was arousing him in ways he'd never believed possible and he had to shift to relieve the discomfort his jeans suddenly caused him.

As her lips moved over his, her hand busily worked at unsnapping the grippers on his shirt. With a pop that sounded like a cannon going off to his heightened senses, first one snap, then another gave way.

She lifted her head and the smile she gave him made him wonder what she had planned next. He didn't have to wait to find out. Leaning over, she began pressing kisses to his newly exposed skin, and with each touch of her lips a tiny charge of electricity shot straight up his spine. But when her tongue darted out to circle his flat nipple, he thought he might just end up being electrocuted from the current coursing through him.

"Darlin', you're killing me."

Her throaty laughter sent a shaft of desire coursing through every cell in his body. "You want me to stop?"

He swallowed hard in an effort to moisten the cotton coating his throat. "Hell no!"

Smiling, she rose to her knees and reached for his belt. "Are you sure?"

When he nodded, she worked the leather strap through the metal buckle, then eased the tab of his fly down. Her fingers brushed against the cotton fabric covering his arousal and he jerked as if he'd been zapped by a cattle prod.

"I can't stand much more of this," he said through gritted teeth. Unable to lie still any longer, he sat up. "It's high time I evened the score."

"What did you have in mind?" she asked, her voice sliding over him like a sensual purr.

"This," he said, pulling her sweatshirt over her head. She was wearing the lacey bra he'd seen through her wet T-shirt the day she'd arrived on the Triple Bar. He ran his finger along the edge of the cup. "You know, as good as you look in this, I like you better out of it."

"You do?"

He nodded and unhooked the closure at the valley of her breasts. Pulling the straps from her shoulders, he tossed the scrap of lace on top of his hat, then filled his hands with her.

"This kind of beauty shouldn't be covered up," he said, lowering his head to take one coral nipple into his mouth. Running his tongue over the tight peak, he tasted her, then sucked the tight bud until she moaned with pleasure. "Does that feel good, darlin'?"

"Mmmm."

"Want me to stop?"

"No." She reached out to trace her fingers over his own puckered flesh. "How does that feel?"

"Good." He closed his eyes as a shudder ran the length of him. "Damned good." When her fingertips skimmed down his chest and belly to the waistband of his briefs, his eyes popped open. "What are you doing now?"

Her smile just about turned him wrong-side out. "Last night you explored my body, now it's my turn to explore yours."

At her urging, he rose to his knees, his heart pounding like a jackhammer against his ribs. "Darlin', there's something you should know."

"What's that?" she asked.

His breathing felt as if he'd been running a marathon and he had to concentrate hard on what he was trying to tell her. "At this stage of the game, I don't think I can stand a whole lot of exploration."

"I'll keep that in mind."

Faith held his gaze with hers as she lifted his hands to place them on her shoulders, then slowly shoved his jeans down to his knees. He felt her fingers slide beneath the elastic band of his briefs and the anticipation of her touch had him gritting his teeth for control. It took everything he had not to rip both of their clothes off and end the sweet torture. But when she gently eased the cotton fabric over his arousal, pushed them down to his thighs, then took him into her soft warm hands, his head felt as if it might come right off his shoulders.

She traced his length and measured his girth while her palm cupped him. The rush of desire that coursed through him made him dizzy.

But when she stroked him, he took her hands in his and shook his head. "Darlin', much more of that and we'll both be sorry."

Passion colored her porcelain cheeks as without a word, she stood up and removed her jeans and panties. He could tell she was as turned on as he was.

When she once again knelt down in front of him, Cooper laid back against the straw. She started to take off his boots, but he wrapped his arms around her and drew her on top of him. Kissing her, he let her know he didn't want to waste time dispensing with the rest of his clothes.

She seemed to understand as she straddled him and guided him to her. He watched her body take him in, felt her melt around him. Closing his eyes, he struggled to hang onto what little control he had left.

Everything in his being was demanding that he thrust within her, to race toward what he knew would be a soul-shattering climax. But taking deep even breaths, he willed his body to slow down. He refused to complete his satisfaction unless he was assured that Faith achieved the same degree of pleasure.

When she rocked against him, he opened his eyes to gaze up at the woman who held him so intimately. She was the most beautiful woman in the world and her body caressing his as she moved was quickly shredding every good intention he possessed.

Grasping her hips, he held on as she rode him to the edge of no return. The red haze of passion surrounded him, blinding him to anything but the intense sensations Faith was drawing from him. Never in his entire life had he felt anything as overwhelming. She possessed him body and soul.

Her moan of pleasure came a moment before he felt her inner muscles quiver then squeeze him as her body urged his complete surrender to hers. His muscles contracted as he thrust into her one final time, and groaning, he gave himself up to her demands as he emptied his seed deep inside of her.

In that moment, he knew without a doubt that he'd surrendered more than just his body to her. He'd just given her all of his heart and soul.

Ten

Seated next to Cooper as he drove the distance between his ranch and the Rocking M, Faith became more apprehensive with each passing mile. She should have made her excuses and stayed behind at the Triple Bar while he visited his sister and her family.

She glanced over at his handsome profile and her chest tightened. Her reluctance to attend the gathering had nothing to do with not wanting to learn more about the man she loved, and everything to do with her self-preservation.

She'd desperately tried to deny the pull between them, tried not to fall in love with him. But Cooper had made it impossible. He was kind, considerate and the most caring man she'd ever met. How could she not fall hopelessly in love with him? Or want to know everything about him?

But the day would come when she'd have to leave the Triple Bar ranch—leave Cooper—and the more deeply involved she became with him and his family, the harder it would be for her when it was time to go. And there was no doubt that she'd have to leave. Cooper wanted things that she could never give him. It would be unfair to him if she stayed and he gave up those dreams for her.

"You're awfully quiet," he said, reaching over to take her hand in his. "Is something bothering you?"

She shook her head. "I'm just a little tired," she lied.

He grinned and her insides felt as if they turned to melted butter. "I shouldn't have kept you awake so long last night."

His reference to their lovemaking caused a flutter deep in the pit of her stomach. "I'm not complaining," she said, trying not to sound as breathless as she felt.

"Good." He kissed the back of her hand. "Because I intend to keep you up late tonight, too."

Her heart rate increased and the fluttering in her stomach increased. She needed to lighten the moment or she might just go into total meltdown right there in the cab of his truck.

"You're insatiable," she said, laughing.

"When it comes to you, I am," he admitted. The look in his eyes seared her and she suddenly felt like fanning herself.

He steered the truck off the main road and as they passed under a wrought iron sign with Rocking M on it, she noticed a black horse grazing contentedly in the neatly kept pasture to their right. "That's a beautiful animal," she said, hoping to distract Cooper's attention.

"That's Jenna's stallion, Black Satin," he said, slowing the truck for her to take a better look. "A few years back he was the national reigning horse champion." He laughed. "Now he's just the well-kept boyfriend of about twenty-five brood mares."

"Your sister raises horses?"

He nodded. "That's how she and Flint met. He owned Black Satin and hired Jenna to train him. But since she's the only person who can do anything with Satin, Flint gave him to her for a wedding present."

"Your sister sounds like she's a very accomplished horsewoman."

"She sure is," he said, sounding proud. Smiling he added, "You two will get along great."

Faith could tell that Cooper was close to his sister and that it was extremely important to him that she meet the woman. Her apprehension increased. He wasn't just taking her to a casual family gathering, he was taking her to get his sister's stamp of approval. Her hands grew cold and a tight knot began to form in her stomach. She had a feeling she was in way over her head.

"We're here," Cooper said, parking the pickup beside an SUV with the Rocking M logo painted on the side.

Lost in thought, Faith failed to notice their approach to the big two-story ranch house. "They have a beautiful home," she commented as he helped her from his truck.

He frowned. "It's a far cry from the Triple Bar, isn't it?"

She knew he was comparing the two places and

finding his sorely lacking. "One day the Triple Bar will be just as nice, if not nicer than this ranch," she said, touching his cheek. "Just remember that."

He turned his head to kiss her palm. "Thanks, darlin'."

Before she could respond, two little boys burst through the back door, bounded down the steps and raced across the yard to greet them.

"Uncle Cooper, you've got to hear what we did in Florida," the older one said. "It was awesome."

"Yeah, awestrom," the little one said, excitedly. He hurled himself at Cooper and giggled delightedly when his uncle swung him up into his arms.

"Faith, I'd like for you to meet my nephews." Cooper ruffled the oldest one's tobacco brown hair. "This is Ryan. He's eight."

Ryan wiped his hand on the seat of his pants, then stuck it out for her to shake. "Nice to meet you, ma'am."

"It's nice to meet you, too, Ryan." She smiled as she shook his hand, marveling at how much he looked like his father, Flint.

"And this little bundle of energy I'm holding is Danny. He's three," Cooper said, shifting the toddler to sit on his arm.

She could see the love in Cooper's eyes, the pleasure of being with the little boys. He would be a wonderful, loving father one day.

Danny's little blond head bobbed up and down with excitement. "Uncle Coopa, I went to Frorida and made a sandcastle."

"Sandcastle," Ryan corrected.

"That's what I said," Danny insisted. "Sand-crastle."

"Most of the time he talks pretty good for a little kid," Ryan explained to Faith. "But he still has trouble with some words."

Thoroughly charmed by both children, Faith smiled. "He's lucky to have a big brother like you to help him out."

"Ryan? Danny?" A pretty blond haired woman stepped out onto the back porch. Spotting Cooper, she grinned. "I should have known you were the reason the boys almost knocked the door off its hinges trying to get outside."

Cooper grinned. "Hey there, little sister. How's life treating you these days?"

"Mom's been real sick," Ryan said, looking worried.

Descending the steps, she walked over to where they stood. "Remember, your dad and I explained this to you the other night," she said patiently as she put a reassuring arm around the child's shoulders. "It's just a temporary thing. I'm going to be fine."

"What's up, sis?" Cooper asked, his grin immediately turning to concern. "Flint mentioned you had some kind of stomach thing when he was over at the Triple Bar the other day."

She nodded. "That's what I thought. But it looks like it's going to last longer than just a few days." Her smile was radiant. "It's nothing that another seven months won't cure."

Faith watched Cooper's easy expression return. "Really?" When she nodded, he put his free arm around her shoulders to hug her. "Congratulations, sis. Will I be getting a niece this time?"

"That's what we're hoping for." Turning to Faith, she smiled apologetically. "I'm sorry. We're being rude. You must be Faith.'' She pointed toward Cooper. ''I'm Jenna McCray, this big lug's sister.''

''I'm pleased to meet you,'' Faith said, nodding. It was completely ridiculous, and she felt ashamed of herself for feeling the way she did, but she couldn't keep a tiny twinge of envy from running through her when she'd learned of Jenna's pregnancy.

''Uncle Cooper, are we gonna hunt for critters?'' Ryan asked, expectantly.

''Wanna hunt kitters,'' Danny agreed, nodding his little blond head.

''It just so happens that Faith found one over at my house the other day and I caught it for you guys,'' he said, setting Danny on his feet.

''Cooper,'' Jenna warned.

''Don't go getting all riled up, sis,'' he said, reaching into the bed of his truck. ''I built a cage for it.''

Faith shuddered when she saw him remove the cage containing the mouse. ''That's one little creature you can have with my blessings.''

Jenna laughed. ''I see we feel the same way about these things.'' To Cooper she said, ''You'll have to find a place for it out in the barn. Under no circumstances is that thing coming inside the house.''

''But, Mom,'' Ryan protested. ''He's just a little guy.''

''Wittle guy, Mommy,'' Danny chimed in.

''It's the barn or nothing,'' Jenna said firmly. Faith couldn't have agreed more with her. She hadn't wanted the little critter in the same house with her either.

Cooper handed the small cage to Ryan. ''You

heard your mom, guys. We'll have to find a place in the barn.''

Jenna hooked her arm through Faith's and turned toward the house. "While Cooper and the boys find a place for the mouse, why don't we go inside and get acquainted? I've got several stories to tell you about that brother of mine."

Faith smiled. She liked Cooper's sister immediately and couldn't wait to hear what the woman had to say about the man Faith loved.

Two hours later, Cooper sat at the big dining room table watching his sister whisper something to Faith. Whatever it was, both women seemed to find it quite humorous.

Even though he had a feeling their amusement was at his expense, it pleased him no end to see that Faith and his sister had hit it off. "What's so funny?" he asked, grinning at the two women who meant the most to him.

Faith gave him a smile that made him glad the tablecloth covered his lap. "Nothing you'd be interested in," she said, giggling.

"Nothing at all." Jenna agreed. She laughed as she wiped Danny's hands and face, then lifted him out of his booster seat.

"Uh-oh, boy," Whiskers said, scooting his chair away from the table. "When womenfolk pack up like that and start to teeheein', you better watch out." He shook his head, his eyes twinkling merrily. "Ryan, you and Danny come with me into the family room and we'll turn on the football game." He shot Cooper a toothless grin. "I have a feelin' when your uncle finds out what your momma's told Miss Faith, it ain't gonna be real purty.''

Both women laughed as if Whiskers had hit the nail on the head.

Cooper frowned. ''I can't think of anything—''

Flint chuckled. ''Let this be your first lesson about women, Coop.'' He reached over to cover Jenna's hand with his where it rested on the top of the table. ''They have minds like steel traps and never forget anything.'' He grinned. ''And you can bet it's something you'd rather forget.''

Faith and Jenna laughed again, making the hair on the back of Cooper's neck stand straight up. Surely Jenna wouldn't mention…

''You didn't,'' he said, narrowing his eyes on his sister.

Jenna's eyes danced as she asked, ''Does Fort Worth ring a bell, big brother?''

Heat crept from beneath his collar, spread up his neck and burned his cheeks. Jenna had told Faith about the time he'd been bucked off, then lost his pants when the bull hooked a horn in his hip pocket and ripped his jeans damned near off of him. He'd left the arena with his jeans in shreds and had to cover his butt with his hat in order to keep from offending anyone's delicate sensibilities.

''One of the Dallas television stations ran the clip on their evening news,'' Jenna said, laughing. ''Then it was picked up by the network.''

''Oh, no!'' Faith was laughing so hard that she had to wipe tears from her eyes.

Jenna nodded. ''The film clip was chosen as a Picture of the Week and broadcast on one of the national news shows.''

When Cooper groaned, Flint threw back his head and laughed. "I told you it would be something you'd like to forget." He rose to his feet to start clearing the table. "Face it, Coop. That little moment in the spotlight will haunt you until the day you die."

His face still feeling like it was on fire, Cooper gladly helped his brother-in-law clear the table. It was either that or strangle his sister for sharing the most embarrassing moment of his life with Faith.

After they'd carried the plates and serving bowls into the kitchen, Cooper returned to the dining room while Flint went into the family room to see how the Cowboys were doing against the 49ers.

"Where's Faith?" he asked when he found Jenna sitting at the table alone.

"Ryan and Danny wanted her to see their turtle."

"Good." He sat down in the chair beside her. "You and I need to talk."

"That's why I'm still sitting here," Jenna said, shifting to face him.

Before he had a chance to think about what he was going to say, he blurted, "I'm in love with her, sis."

"I can tell."

He grinned. "Is it that obvious?"

Smiling, she nodded. "And she's in love with you."

Warmth spread throughout his body at the thought that Faith cared as much for him as he did for her. "You think so?"

"I know so." Jenna wrapped her arms around his shoulders to give him a huge hug. "I'm happy for you, Cooper. She's a wonderful person and I'm looking forward to having her for a sister-in-law. It looks like Whiskers's meddling worked out for the best.''

Pulling away from her, Cooper shook his head. ''I'm not so sure it will work out.''

Jenna looked puzzled. ''Why? You both love each other.''

''This isn't a good time right now for me to be thinking in terms of forever,'' he admitted. ''The ranch isn't even close to being what I want it to be.''

''So what does that have to do with anything?'' she asked, clearly puzzled.

''Think about it, Jenna. I don't have a thing to offer Faith right now.'' He shook his head. ''Hell, the house doesn't even have plumbing.''

''And you think she hasn't already noticed that?'' his sister asked dryly. Her expression turned serious. ''Cooper, you're forgetting something here.''

''What's that?''

''Faith has lived there with you for the past week and a half. She knows exactly what needs to be done to the ranch. And she's still there.'' Placing her hand on his shoulder, Jenna smiled as she stood up. ''Don't you see? It doesn't matter to her. She loves you for you, not for what the ranch will be one day.''

''But I wanted to—''

Jenna shook her head. ''Build it together, Cooper. Let her help you and it will become her dream, too.''

When Jenna walked into the kitchen, he thought about what she'd said. Maybe she was right. Faith had seen the ranch at its worst and had turned down the opportunity to leave, not once, but twice.

And she believed in him and his ability to turn the Triple Bar around. It hadn't been more than a couple of hours ago that she'd told him his ranch would be just as nice if not nicer than the Rocking M one day.

His chest tightened. He loved Faith more than life itself and there was no doubt in his mind that he wanted to spend the rest of his days with her. Now all he had to do was find the perfect time to ask her to share his life, his dream.

"Cooper, do you think we should be getting back to the Triple Bar?" Faith asked as she and Jenna walked into the dining room together. "Penelope will be wanting to eat by the time we get back."

Leaning over, Jenna kissed his cheek. "You take care, big brother." Then in a soft whisper, added, "See what I mean? Let her work with you and the reality will be far better than the dream could ever be."

"Do you need my help?" Cooper asked, setting the bucket of warm water on the bench in the feed room.

Faith laughed and shook her head. "Penelope and I have a very effective system worked out. I hold onto the bucket for dear life and she drains it." Faith measured out the amount of formula, then poured it into the nursing bucket. "If you have something you need to do, go ahead. We'll be fine."

"Thanks," he said, brushing a kiss across her forehead. He gave her a smile that curled her toes, then without another word, he turned and disappeared through the doorway.

She stirred water into the powdered milk and wondered what demanded his immediate attention this time. There was no telling. After observing the work he put into the daily care and feeding of the cattle and horses, it could be one of a dozen different chores.

Shrugging, she carried the nippled bucket to Penelope's stall. She didn't mind that he was too busy to talk to her while she fed the calf. It gave her time to reflect on her day at the McCray ranch.

Even though she'd been reluctant to meet Cooper's family, she'd really enjoyed getting acquainted with them. She'd told herself to keep her distance and not form any attachments—that it would just make things that much harder for her when the time came for her to go back to Illinois. But they'd made it impossible not to care for them. Jenna had been so nice and friendly that Faith felt like they'd been friends for years. And the boys were such adorable little imps, she couldn't help but fall in love with them.

Lost in thought, Faith almost dropped the bucket when Penelope butted against it. Looking down, she was amazed to see that the calf had drunk almost all of the formula.

"Looks like she was pretty hungry," Cooper said, walking into the stall.

Faith glanced up. "Did you get your chores done?"

"I finished those before we left this morning," he said, smiling.

She looked down at the bucket. "I'm finished feeding Penelope. Did you need my help with something?"

He nodded and the sexy grin on his handsome face nearly melted her bones. Taking the bucket from her, he took hold of her hand, led her out of the stall, then secured the door to keep Penelope from getting out. "I need you to come with me."

"Where are we going?" she asked, laughing.

"You'll see." They remained silent as they walked through the early evening twilight to the house, but when they reached the back steps, he stopped and set the nursing bucket on the porch. "Close your eyes, darlin'."

"Why?"

His grin made her heart skip a beat. "Because I want to surprise you."

"What on earth have you got up your sleeve this time?" she asked, breathlessly. The last time he'd made a request like this, she'd ended up learning to dance. Her heart fluttered when she thought of how that evening had ended.

"Do you trust me, Faith?" he asked. His low voice sent a shiver up her spine and caused her knees to wobble.

"You know I do," she said without hesitation. It still amazed her how easily she'd placed her trust in him. Maybe it had been the integrity in his deep blue eyes, or his gentle, caring manner. She wasn't sure. But she knew beyond a shadow of doubt that Cooper would never do anything to hurt her in any way.

"Then close yours eyes, darlin'."

When she did as he requested, he took her hand and carefully guided her up the steps and into the house. She could tell they were moving beyond the kitchen and down the hall.

"Where are we going?" she asked as he led her through the house.

He came to a stop. "Right here."

"Can I open my eyes?" she asked, laughing.

"In just a minute."

She heard him move away from her, then the sounds of the CD with slow country songs—the one that she'd come to love—floated through the air. "Cooper?"

"Open your eyes, darlin'," he said, from beside her.

The living room was once again illuminated with candles and the packing carton he'd used as a table the night they'd danced had been set for two. A platter of bite-size cheese squares sat in the middle of it and two wine goblets with a rich red wine sat at each place.

Turning, she wrapped her arms around his neck and kissed him. "You're the most romantic man I've ever known."

Looking a little embarrassed, he shook his head. "Nah, I just wanted to do something a little special for you."

She didn't think she could possibly love him any more than she did at that moment. In all of their four-year marriage, Eric had never done anything as thoughtful.

"How did you bring all this from the Rocking M without my seeing it?" she asked as he seated her at the makeshift table.

He shrugged and sat down on the crate beside her. "Jenna loaned me a cooler and while you were saying goodbye to everyone, I loaded it into the back of the truck."

"I'll have to thank her the next time I see her," she said, picking up a piece of cheese. Something was different about him, but she couldn't put a finger on what it was.

When she held the cheese to his mouth, his gaze caught and held hers as he took it from her, then nibbled at her fingers with his lips. A tingling warmth filled her and ended all speculation.

He smiled. "I'm the one who should be thanking you for everything you've done around here, darlin'." He drew her finger into his mouth and gently sucked on it before letting it go.

"M-me? I haven't done anything but get…in your way most of the time," she said, reaching for her wine goblet. Her hand trembled and she hoped taking a sip of her wine would help steady her voice.

"That's where you're wrong, Faith." He held a piece of cheese for her to sample, then traced her lips with his index finger. "You've held boards, worked to get the house cleaned up and taken better care of Penelope than her own momma would have done."

How was she supposed to concentrate on chewing the cheese he'd given her when his fingertips touching her lips were causing all kinds of delicious sensations to be unleashed deep inside of her?

"I've…enjoyed helping out," she said, breathlessly.

He reached for her hand, then kissed the back of it. "And I've enjoyed having you here with me."

His smooth baritone and sexy grin only added to the warm tingling in the pit of her stomach. But when she gazed into his eyes, her heart skipped several beats and she realized what was different about him. His desire for her was there, as it had been almost from the moment they met. But this time there was also love shining in the dark blue depths.

Her breath came out in soft little puffs. "C-Cooper?"

He took the wineglass from her, set it on the table, then stood up to gather her into his arms. Gazing down at her, he lowered his mouth to hers with such tenderness, her knees failed to support her.

Sagging against him, she gave herself up to his soul-shattering kiss and forgot all about the reason the look of love in his eyes scared her to death. Or that the time had come for her to leave the Triple Bar Ranch.

Eleven

Cooper steadied Faith, then walked over to blow out the candles. Coming back to stand in front of her, he swung her up into his arms and headed for the bedroom.

He'd intended to ask her to share his future, to stay with him and become his wife. But the moment he'd taken her into his arms, the need to possess her, to once again make her his, had become too great a force to resist. He'd never in his life wanted a woman more than he did Faith at that very moment. There would be plenty of time to ask her to marry him after they made love.

Entering the bedroom, he placed her on the bed. His hands shook, but he somehow managed to dispense with their clothing, then stretched out beside her and gathered her back into his arms. He couldn't get enough of touching her, of feeling her body tremble with need for him.

He wanted to tell Faith how much he loved her, but incapable of words, he lowered his mouth to hers and showed her what was in his heart, what was burning in his soul. She opened for him and the tentative touch of her tongue to his created a flash fire, searing every nerve in his body, branding him as hers.

The blood raced through his veins and his pulse pounded in his ears as her hands slid over his chest and flanks. It was as if she were trying to learn every nuance of his body, trying to commit him to memory.

"Easy, darlin'," he said, gently pushing her back on the mattress. "If we don't slow down, I'm not going to last much longer."

Gazing down into her luminous brown eyes, he saw a burning desperation that he'd never seen in them before. He fleetingly wondered why it felt as if this would be their final time together, as if they were saying goodbye. But he threw off the ridiculous feeling and concentrated on bringing her pleasure, showing her with his body what mere words could never express.

Lowering his head, he kissed his way from her collarbone down the slope of her breast to the taut peak. He took the coral nipple into his mouth, teasing, tasting. When she shivered with passion, he gently chafed her wet skin with the pad of his thumb as he moved to pay homage to the other tight nub.

"So sweet," he murmured, when she moaned and clutched at his hair with her hands.

Pleased that she enjoyed his attention, he trailed kisses down her stomach to the tiny indention at her waist and beyond. His body throbbed with need, but he ignored it. This was all for Faith, all about showing her how much he loved her.

He smoothed his hands down her hips and legs, then drew them up along her inner thighs to the soft nest of curls hiding her feminine secrets. Nudging her knees apart, he moved to learn all of her, to give her pleasure in the most selfless way a man could possibly give to a woman.

''Cooper—''

The sound of his name on her passion-filled voice encouraged him and he cupped her hips with his hands to steady their restless movements. Bending down to kiss her in the most intimate of ways, he continued the sensual assault until she cried out and shuddered with the ecstasy of completion.

Moving to her side, he held her close and kissed her with every emotion he had coursing through him. But instead of lying passively in his arms as her body cooled, Faith reached out to touch him, to hold him in her hands and stroke him with a tenderness that made him dizzy with wanting.

Her gentle hands caressing him, testing his strength, was heaven and hell rolled into one. He wanted nothing more than to bury himself deep inside of her, to claim her as his own. But he sensed her need to express her feelings for him, to show him the same attention that he'd shown her.

As her lips moved over his chest and belly his pulse pounded in his ears and he had to force himself to breathe. But when she took him into her mouth, time stood still as wave after wave of desire flowed through him. Heat and light danced behind his tightly closed eyes and his world narrowed to one purpose—complete release.

"Darlin', I can't stand any more of this," he said, lifting her up to his chest.

Taking deep breaths, he willed his body to slow down, to relax until he'd gained control once again. But the feel of her softness pressed to him, the warmth of her breath on his heated skin, tested him in ways he'd never imagined.

"Cooper, please make love to me," she said, her voice wrapping around him like a velvet sheath.

He might have been able to hang onto what little scrap of sanity he had left had it not been for her softly spoken request. But knowing that she wanted him as much as he wanted her snapped the last thread of his restraint and he rolled her to her back, then covered her body with his.

At the first touch of her moist heat to his insistent arousal, he clenched his teeth so hard his jaw felt as if it would break from the pressure. Slowly, carefully he pushed forward until he lost sight of where he ended and she began.

Her moan of pleasure and the feel of himself buried deep inside of her created a sensual fog of passion that clouded his brain to anything but the act of bringing them the satisfaction they both craved.

Thrusting deeply, thoroughly, he felt her feminine muscles contract around him, holding him tightly to her, urging him to empty himself deep into her womb. Gratified by the sound of her broken cries, he groaned as the whirlwind of sensation caught him in its grasp and he gave himself to the only woman he'd ever loved.

Several moments passed before he found the

strength to move to her side, then pull her to him. Brushing a strand of hair from her eyes, his heart stalled at the moisture he felt on her smooth cheek.

If he'd hurt her in any way he'd never be able to forgive himself. "Faith? Darlin', what's wrong? Are you all right?"

"That was beautiful," she said, softly.

He relaxed. She was having one of those emotional female moments that women sometimes had, and that a man couldn't even begin to understand.

Smiling, he kissed the top of her head. "I love you, Faith Broderick."

"And I love you, Cooper Adams," she said passionately. "More than you'll ever know."

His heart soared. She loved him. He felt like he could move a mountain with his bare hands.

"Marry me, darlin'. Let me love you to sleep every night and wake up with you every morning." He raised up to look down at her. "I want to be the man who gives you your babies, Faith. And I want to be there by your side when you birth them."

Tears streamed from her eyes as she stared up at him, then throwing her arms around his neck, she hugged him tightly to her. "Oh, Cooper."

She hadn't said "yes" exactly, but he took her emotional response and the fact that she was holding him like she'd never let him go as a good sign. Content with the knowledge that she loved him, and confident that they'd be getting married in the very near future, he relaxed and felt the exhaustion from their lovemaking overtake him.

"Get some rest now, darlin'," he said, cradling her to his chest. He yawned. "We can start making plans first thing in the morning."

* * *

Faith's tears continued long after Cooper's deep, even breathing signaled that he'd fallen asleep. She'd tried so hard not to love him, tried to keep her distance.

But as impossible as it had been for her not to fall in love with Cooper, it had become just as impossible for her to stay with him.

She'd seen him interact with his nephews and heard him talk about how much he loved being around kids. He'd even told her he wanted a large family. And if ever a man deserved being a father, Cooper Adams did.

But what he didn't deserve was a wife who couldn't give him those children. And as desperately as she wanted to be his wife and have his babies, to be part of the family he so desired, she simply couldn't do it. Her body just wasn't capable.

She and Eric had tried for over a year to become pregnant, but with no success. At first she'd thought it might be something with him. But when she confided her fears in her best friend, Charlotte, Faith had learned that it wasn't Eric's problem at all. It was hers. Charlotte had fallen in love with Eric and become pregnant with his baby, and Faith had not only been forced to face the betrayal of her husband and best friend, she'd been confronted with the devastating reality that she was infertile. They'd both apologized, but that didn't alter the fact that they had everything she'd always wanted, but could never have.

That's why she had to leave Cooper now. She knew him well enough to know that he'd say it wasn't important, that they would have each other and that was all that mattered. But as much as she'd like to ignore the facts and stay with him for the rest of her life, Cooper deserved to have his dream, his family.

And she loved him enough not to take that away from him.

She bit her lower lip to stifle a sob and held him close for a few moments longer. Then kissing his lean cheek one last time, she slipped from his embrace and got out of bed.

Gathering her things, she quickly got dressed and carried her luggage out to his truck. For the first time since her arrival on the ranch, she was glad that she hadn't had a place to put her clothes. Living out of a suitcase had been extremely inconvenient, but it saved precious time that she couldn't afford to waste now.

Taking a notepad and a pen from her purse, she turned on the dome light and with tears blurring her vision, she explained on paper what she didn't have the courage to tell him face-to-face.

She wasn't proud of what she was doing, but she knew that for both of their sakes, leaving this way was the only option. Cooper would try to talk her into staying, and loving him as she did, she'd be powerless to resist.

Carefully folding the paper, she wrote his name on the outside, then placed it on the bench seat beside her. Wiping the moisture from her face, she took a deep breath and started the truck. Once she reached the airport in Amarillo, she'd call Whiskers and have him see about getting Cooper's truck back to him.

* * *

His eyes still closed, Cooper rolled over to pull Faith into his arms, to love her awake. But the bed was empty beside him, the sheets cold.

He opened one eye and groaned. A bright shaft of sunlight was streaming through the window. Damn. He'd overslept again.

Stretching, he thought about the chores that needed to be done, then shook his head. What he really wanted to do was find Faith, bring her back to bed and make love to her for the rest of the day.

He briefly wondered why she hadn't awakened him. They had a lot to do. Not only did they have to take care of the usual chores, they had a wedding to plan.

Grinning at the thought of making her his wife, he swung his legs over the side of the bed and reaching for his clothes, froze. The corner of the room where he'd stacked her suitcases the day after she'd arrived was empty.

Where was Faith's luggage?

Apprehension gnawed at his gut as he quickly pulled on his clothes and hurried down the hall. "Faith?"

The ominous silence in the house was deafening.

When he entered the kitchen, he looked for the CD player, her book, anything that said she was still there.

He found nothing.

Throwing open the back door, he stepped out onto the porch just as his truck drove into the yard. But instead of Faith, Whiskers got out of the cab.

"Where is she?" Cooper demanded. He dreaded the answer, but he had to know.

For the first time since he'd known the old man, Whiskers seemed at a loss for words. He simply

walked up to the porch, handed Cooper a folded
piece of paper, then shaking his head, started toward
the barn.

A sinking feeling tightened Cooper's chest as he
noticed his name on the outside. The handwriting
was a woman's. It had to be Faith's.

His hands shook as he opened the note, read it,
then carefully refolded it and stuck it in his shirt
pocket. Anger burned at his gut and he had a deep
need to shout his frustration.

He could have understood Faith's leaving him because of the condition of the ranch, or out of fear
that he could adequately provide for her. But for her
to abandon what they had together because she
couldn't have kids was unacceptable.

"Damn fool woman."

Did she honestly think he was that shallow? Did
she really believe that he wanted kids more than he
wanted her?

He took a deep breath, then another as his words
came back to haunt him. After they'd made love last
night, he'd asked her to marry him, then immediately
started talking about them having a family together.

He shook his head at his own stupidity. He'd just
the same as told her that's why he wanted to marry
her. But if she thought he was going to let a little
thing like her not being able to have a baby stop him
from being with the only woman he'd ever loved,
she was in for a big surprise.

Pulling his cell phone from the holder on the side
of his belt, he punched in Brant Wakefield's number.
After he'd explained what he needed, Cooper ended
the call, then descended the steps and walked out to
the barn.

"Whiskers, I have a job for you," he said when he spotted the old man standing outside of Penelope's stall.

"What's that, boy?" Whiskers asked, his tone cautious.

"For the next two weeks, I need you here to cook meals for about five men."

"That sounds fair 'nuff," Whiskers said, nodding. "What you got planned?"

"I've got a pasture to fence, a house to rewire and plumbing to put in."

Whiskers looked shocked. "That's it? You ain't gonna—"

When the old geezer's voice trailed off, Cooper almost laughed. He could tell that curiosity was about to kill Whiskers. The man couldn't figure out why Cooper wasn't more upset about Faith's leaving.

Taking pity on his old friend, Cooper explained, "After I get this place in shape, I have a little trip to take."

"A trip?" Whiskers's face lit up brighter than a Christmas tree full of lights. "And jest where you goin', Coop?"

Cooper grinned. "I thought I'd take a ride up to Illinois and see if I couldn't find myself a good woman to settle down with."

Whiskers laughed. "I was beginnin' to wonder 'bout you, boy."

"I don't give up that easy," Cooper said, shaking his head. He smiled at the man whose meddling had helped him find the woman of his dreams. "I know what I want. And I'm damned well not afraid to go after her."

Twelve

"I'm what?!"

"I said you're pregnant, Ms. Broderick."

Faith stared at the woman in total disbelief. "That's not possible. My ex-husband and I tried for over a year and we never could get pregnant. And I *know* he wasn't the one with the problem. He and his wife have a child now."

"In some cases the harder a couple tries, the less successful they are," Dr. Shelton said, smiling. "Sometimes all it takes is for them to relax and stop worrying about becoming pregnant."

Faith thought back on her marriage. Once she and Eric had made the decision to try to have a baby, he'd started keeping graphs and charts of everything from her temperature to the best time of the month for them to make love. And with each month they were unsuccessful, it added more stress and tension to their relationship.

The doctor handed her a prescription for prenatal vitamins as she rose to leave. ''I want you to cut out caffeine, get plenty of rest, eat well-balanced meals and take these.'' She patted Faith's shoulder. ''Congratulations. I'm sure once the shock wears off, you'll be very happy.''

As Faith got dressed, a thousand different things ran through her mind. She was going to have a baby. Unbelievable!

She'd attributed her feeling lousy for the past couple of weeks to missing Cooper, and of second-guessing her decision to leave the Triple Bar ranch every minute of every day since she'd come home.

A warm happiness suffused her whole body. She was pregnant with Cooper's baby. She wanted to shout it from the rooftops.

Walking out to the car, she stopped in the middle of the parking lot as a disturbing thought intruded. What if he was so upset with her that he never wanted to see her again?

Fear began to take hold. It had been over two weeks and she'd heard nothing from him. Not a phone call. Not a letter. Nothing.

What if he'd decided she wasn't the woman he wanted after all? Had her judgment once again proven faulty?

She took a deep breath and shoved her doubts aside. She may have been wrong about many things in her life and misplaced her trust in several people, but in her heart, she knew she wasn't wrong about Cooper.

In her note to him, she'd asked that he not try to

contact her. Maybe he had just been respecting her wishes.

Getting into the driver's seat of her grandmother's car, she pulled the visor down and gazed into the vanity mirror. She didn't look any different than she had this morning when she was getting ready for her doctor's appointment. But in the past forty-five minutes her whole life had changed. Forever.

She was having a baby. Cooper's baby.

For the first time in two weeks she felt a bubble of hope begin to rise within her.

Cooper pulled the rental car away from the Williamson County Airport and, following a map, easily found the little town of Carterville. He was glad he'd made the decision to fly instead of drive the nine-hundred-plus miles to Faith's grandmother's place. It would have taken him more time than he was willing to waste and been one more day without Faith in his arms.

Less than five minutes after he drove into town, he was standing on the front porch of Faith's grand-mother's home, knocking on the door.

When an older lady answered the door, he smiled. "Is this where Faith Broderick lives?"

Her gaze raked him from the top of his Resistol to the soles of his boots before she nodded. "You must be Cooper Adams."

Hoping it was a good sign that Faith had mentioned him to her grandmother, his smile turned to a grin. "Yes, ma'am. I sure am."

"I'm Faith's grandmother, Penelope Hudson," she said, shaking his hand.

"Is Faith home, Mrs. Hudson? I need to discuss some things with her."

She shook her head. "I'm sorry. Faith is gone right now, but she should be back soon."

"Would you mind if I waited for her, ma'am? It's really important that I talk to her."

The woman smiled pleasantly for the first time since he'd knocked on the door. "Why don't you come in and have a cup of coffee, son? It'll give us the chance to get acquainted."

"I'd like that, ma'am," Cooper said as he stepped through the opened door. "I'd like that a lot."

When Faith returned from the doctor's office, a car she'd never seen before blocked the drive. She fleetingly wondered who could be visiting, but as she parked her grandmother's Buick along the curb in front of the house, she forgot all about the visitor's identity. She had more important things on her mind.

She needed to call the airlines and reserve a seat on the first available flight to Amarillo. Then, while she packed, she'd need to decide on what she wanted to say to Cooper when she got there.

Mentally ticking off the things she'd need to accomplish before she left, she opened the front door, dropped the car keys on the antique library table in the living room, then walked straight to her bedroom. She heard voices and the sound of laughter coming from the kitchen, but she couldn't tell who was talking or what they were saying.

It didn't matter. She had too much on her mind to worry about who was visiting or what they were discussing. At the moment all she could think of was getting back to Cooper, trying to decide what she would say to him, and hoping that he loved her enough to give them a second chance.

But first things first. She had to find her datebook with the phone number of the airline so she could book her flight. Searching her desk and nightstand, her impatience mounted. It was nowhere to be found. Where could she have put it?

Maybe she'd left it in the living room. She hurried down the hall to search the end tables. No luck there.

"Nana, have you seen my datebook?" she called as she pulled out the couch cushions to see if it had slipped between them.

"Is this what you're looking for?" a rich baritone asked from behind her.

Whirling around, Faith gasped. She couldn't believe her eyes. There stood Cooper casually leaning one shoulder against the door frame, his arms crossed over his chest. In one hand he held her datebook.

"When...did you get here?" she asked, feeling as if she might hyperventilate.

He checked his watch. "About half an hour ago."

Her heart thumped against her ribs and she took a deep breath in an effort to calm herself. His presence dominated the room, and although she'd have never believed it possible, he seemed even more overwhelmingly masculine than ever before.

"Faith, honey, I'm going to the library," her grandmother said, breezing past them on her way to the door. "I just remembered that I promised Phyllis that I would help her sort through some books for the book fair." Turning to Cooper, she smiled. "There's plenty of coffee left if you'd like another cup."

Faith watched Nana scoop the car keys off the small table by the door and walk out, leaving her alone with Cooper.

What was she going to say to him?

She'd thought she'd have several hours to plan what she wanted to tell him first, to prepare herself for seeing him again. But with him standing there looking so handsome, so undeniably male, she could barely remember her own name.

"I could use more coffee," he said, handing her the datebook. He turned to go back into the kitchen. "You want some?"

"No, thank you," she said, remembering the doctor's warning about caffeine. Feeling completely off-center, she tossed the planner onto the couch and followed him.

She watched him walk to the coffeemaker on the counter beside the sink. Pouring himself a cup, he leaned back against the counter, crossed his feet at the ankles and took a sip. "You look tired, darlin'. Why don't you sit down?"

Her knees turned to rubber and her heart skipped a beat at his use of the familiar endearment. Deciding it might not be a bad idea to sit down before she melted in a puddle at his big booted feet, she sank into a chair at the table.

Not knowing what to say, she asked, "How is Penelope?"

He shrugged. "She's doing pretty well, all things considered."

Alarmed, Faith sat up straight. "What do you mean? Has something happened to her?"

"No." He shook his head, then pinned her with his piercing blue gaze. "She's doing fine if you take into consideration that she's been abandoned twice."

"Twice?"

Nodding, he set his cup on the counter, then walked over to stand in front of her. "The first time couldn't be helped. Her momma got stuck in the mud and died before anyone found her. But the second time was an entirely different story.''

Faith gulped. ''I...I'm sorry. At the time I didn't think how it would affect Penelope.''

He pulled out the chair across from her and sat down. ''There were a lot of things you failed to think about, darlin'.''

Leaning back, he looked deceptively relaxed. But she could detect the underlying tension in the tone of his voice, the tiny lines at the corners of his eyes.

''I did what I thought was best,'' she said, defensively. ''I know how much you love children and I didn't want to deprive you of—''

''You don't know squat,'' he said, cutting her explanation short. ''Where do you get off deciding you know what's best for me? Don't you think I'm capable of making those decisions for myself?''

Taken aback, she stammered, ''Well...I...I—''

Sitting forward, he reached across the table to take her hand in his. ''What makes you think I'd rather have children than have you, Faith?''

Speechless, she shook her head.

His smile was so tender it took her breath. ''Don't you know that you can't miss what you've never had?'' He rubbed his thumb over the back of her hand, sending a shiver up her spine. ''But I have had you. And I can't live without you, darlin'.''

''But—'' For the first time since she'd seen him, the hope that had formed earlier when she was leaving the doctor's office began to grow.

He shook his head. ''No 'buts' about it. As long as I have you, it doesn't matter to me if we can't have kids. It's you and your love that I need. Kids would have been an extension of that love, but it wouldn't have been the reason for how I feel about you.'' He smiled. ''If you'd like, someday we can check into adoption. Or if we feel the need from time to time for some real chaos in our lives, we'll borrow Jenna and Flint's kids for a day or two.''

''There's something you need to know, Cooper.''

She watched his jaw tighten and his eyes narrow. ''Do you love me?''

''Yes,'' she said without a moment's hesitation.

''Then there's not another damned thing that matters, darlin','' he said firmly. ''I love you and I want you with me for the rest of my life.'' He lifted her hand to his mouth and brushing her palm with his lips, added, ''I came to take you back to the Triple Bar Ranch where you belong.''

Tears suddenly flooded her eyes and ran down her cheeks as she left her chair and hurled herself into his arms.

Cooper wasn't sure whether to take her emotional outburst as a good sign or not. But at the moment she was in his arms and that was all that mattered.

Holding her close he stroked her hair and murmured what he hoped were soothing words as her emotions ran their course. When her sobs quieted, he lowered his head to kiss her, but leaning back, she shook her head.

''You're wrong, Cooper.''

''You won't go back to Texas with me?'' Was she reluctant to return because she thought life on the ranch would be as primitive as it had been two weeks ago? ''If you're worried about the living conditions, you can stop. You wouldn't recognize the place now.

For the last two weeks I've worked my butt off to get it into shape.''

"Cooper, darling, I'm not worried about that." The smile she gave him just about knocked his size thirteens right off his feet. "There's something else we have to discuss," she said, placing her hand on his cheek.

"What do you want to talk about?" he asked huskily. The feel of her soft hand touching him, caressing him, sent a shaft of desire straight through to his core. He'd like nothing more than to rip their clothes off and prove to her that they belonged together, to once again make her his.

"Since I left Texas, circumstances have changed."

Fear jolted him out of his sensual daydream. "You want to fill me in on what's different?"

He watched her take a deep breath before meeting his eyes. "I told you that I'd been married before."

"Yes, but what has that got to do with—"

She held up her hand. "Let me explain."

As he nodded that he would keep quiet, the fear within him intensified. Was she trying to tell him that she had reconciled with her ex-husband?

"When Eric and I were married, we tried for over a year to get pregnant with no luck. Then just before we were scheduled to go in for testing, I confided in my best friend that I thought Eric might be sterile." She shook her head. "That's when I found out that my husband and best friend had been having an affair and he wasn't the one with the fertility problem."

"He'd gotten her pregnant?" If Cooper could have gotten his hands on the jerk at that moment, he would have cheerfully choked him for hurting Faith.

She nodded. "Eric said that he never meant for it

to happen, but since it had, he wanted to marry Charlotte so he could be with the child I obviously couldn't give him. That's why I quit teaching. We were all teachers at the same school. I just couldn't face being with them day after day and not think about what they had that I couldn't.''

Anger burned in Cooper's gut at the betrayal Faith had suffered at her husband and best friend's hands. But he didn't understand what that had to do with circumstances changing between them. ''What has that got to do with us, darlin'?''

She rose from his lap to pace the floor. Something had her as nervous as a priest in a harem.

''Since it was clear that I was the one with the fertility problem, I didn't see the need to keep the appointment for the testing.'' She bit her lower lip. ''At that point in my life, I just couldn't face having a doctor confirm what I already knew.''

He nodded. ''That's understandable.''

Taking a deep breath, she turned to face him. ''But I was wrong, Cooper.''

His scalp tingled and he sat up straight in the chair. ''About what?'' he asked, slowly.

She laughed nervously. ''It seems I'm not only capable of becoming pregnant, I am pregnant.''

He left the chair so fast it fell over backward on the floor. Cupping her cheeks with his hands, he tilted her face up to meet his gaze. ''Darlin', are you sure?''

''Yes. That's why I was gone when you arrived. I had a doctor's appointment.''

Groaning, Cooper pulled her into his arms and held her close. ''I love you with all my heart and it wouldn't matter to me if you couldn't get pregnant.''

He took a deep breath as emotion tightened his chest. "But I'd be a damned liar if I told you I wasn't the happiest man alive right now, just knowing that you're carrying my baby."

Her arms wrapped around him like she'd never let him go, she asked, "Does the offer still hold?"

"The offer?" Confused, he leaned back to look down at her. "What are you talking about, darlin'?"

"You offered to take me back to the Triple Bar," she said, looking hopeful.

"Nope."

"No?"

Shaking his head, he grinned. "It never was an offer. An offer can be turned down, and I wasn't about to go back to Texas without you." He kissed her with every emotion he had welling up inside of him, then lifting his head, added, "And when we board that plane to go home, you can count on it being as husband and wife."

"You sound rather sure of yourself," she said, giving him a smile that made his body hard with wanting.

"I am sure." He pressed himself to her, letting her know what she did to him, how much he wanted her. "Darlin', I can't promise you I'll be with you for the rest of your life, but you can count on me being with you for the rest of mine."

"I'm going to hold you to that, cowboy." She kissed him and he felt like he'd been given the most precious gift on earth. "I love you, Cooper Adams."

"And I love you, darlin'," he said, swinging her up into his arms. "That's something else you can count on for the rest of my life."

Epilogue

"**W**here Mommy?" Dusty asked, looking around. He clutched a pink bunny in one arm, while he rested his other arm on his father's shoulders.

"She's in a room upstairs with your new baby sister," Cooper said, glancing at his son as he carried him through the hospital lobby.

"Baby Kadie," Dusty said seriously, nodding his little blond head.

An overwhelming sense of love and pride filled Cooper. At a little over two years old, Dustin Cooper Adams was talking better than most kids his age. Of course, as far as Cooper was concerned, Dusty was just about the smartest two-year-old there ever was.

"That's right, your baby sister's name is Katie," Cooper said, smiling. "And we're going to take her and Mommy home with us later today."

Dusty squirmed where he sat on Cooper's arm. "Walk, Daddy. Walk."

Cooper set his son on his feet, straightened his little cowboy hat, then took hold of his hand to keep him from wandering off. "Hang on to Katie's rabbit," he reminded as they stepped onto the elevator.

A few moments later, Cooper led Dusty down the hall and into Faith's room. As soon as he saw his mother, Dusty worked his hand free from Cooper's and ran over to where she sat in a chair holding the baby.

"Mommy!" He held out the pink rabbit. "Dis Kadie's."

"Oh, I'm sure she'll love it, sweetie," Faith said, putting her arm around her son to hug him to her side. "I'm so glad to see you."

Leaning down, Cooper tenderly kissed his wife. "How's the two prettiest girls in the Panhandle?"

Faith smiled up at him. "We're doing just fine. And how did my boys manage on their own last night and this morning?"

"We did pretty good." Cooper smiled down at the most beautiful woman he'd ever known. Although he'd have never believed it possible to love her more than he had three years ago, it didn't even come close to the way he felt for her today. "Dusty helped me feed Penelope and her new calf this morning, didn't you, son?"

Dusty nodded. "Penpee eat lots."

Sensing that his son needed time with his mother, Cooper took the baby, then cradling Katie in one arm, lifted Dusty onto Faith's lap. As Dusty told his mother all about his adventures, Cooper sat down on the side of the bed to get better acquainted with his new daughter.

Katie Jo Adams was the most beautiful little girl he'd ever seen, and when she got older she'd have the boys lined up for miles just to see her smile. Cooper's gut burned at the thought. Now he understood why his brother-in-law, Flint, was so protective of his and Jenna's little girl, Molly.

"It looks like Katie is going to be a daddy's girl," Faith said softly as she held her sleeping son against her breast.

"You think so?" Cooper asked, grinning.

Nodding, Faith smiled at the man she loved with all her heart. She couldn't believe how full her life had become since that day three years ago when she'd found herself stranded with the sexiest man she'd ever seen.

"Thank you, Cooper."

He looked confused. "What did I do?"

"You've given me so much." She glanced down at her son, then at her new daughter. "You've given me your love and two beautiful children." She grinned. "And in a couple of years you can give me another one."

"Darlin', you've just had a baby and you're talking about wanting another one?" he asked, sounding incredulous.

She nodded. "I think another son and daughter would be nice."

"Four kids," he said, seeming to mull it over. He looked down at the baby, then back at Faith, his handsome face troubled. "If you don't mind, I think I'd rather have two more boys."

"Why?" He'd been insistent from the time they

found out she was pregnant with Katie that it would be a girl.

He grimaced. "I'm getting an ulcer just thinking about some pimply-faced kid wanting to take Katie out on a date when she gets older. I don't know if I can handle worrying about two daughters."

"You'll do fine," Faith assured him. "So we're in agreement then? Two more children?"

"Darlin', you can count on me to give you as many babies as you want," he said, his grin wide.

Happier than she'd ever been in her entire life, Faith smiled at her husband. "I love you, Cooper."

"I love you, too, darlin'." The emotion she saw in his eyes took her breath. "That's something you can always count on."

* * * * *

*Be sure to catch Kathie DeNosky's
next Silhouette Desire,
A LAWMAN IN HER STOCKING,
coming in November 2002.*

Silhouette Desire®

presents

DYNASTIES: THE CONNELLYS

A brand-new miniseries about the Connellys of Chicago, a wealthy, powerful American family tied by blood to the royal family of the island kingdom of Altaria. They're wealthy, powerful and rocked by scandal, betrayal…and passion!

Look for a whole year of glamorous and utterly romantic tales in 2002:

Silhouette®
Where love comes alive™

Have you ever wanted to participate in a romance reading group?

Silhouette Special Edition's exciting new book club!

Don't miss

RYAN'S PLACE
by Sherryl Woods

coming in September

Get your friends or relatives together to engage in lively discussions with the suggested reading group questions provided at the end of the novel. Also, visit www.readersring.com for more reading group information!

Available at your favorite retail outlet.

Silhouette®
Where love comes alive™

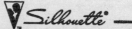

COMING NEXT MONTH

#1459 RIDE THE THUNDER—Lindsay McKenna
Morgan's Mercenaries: Ultimate Rescue
Lieutenant Nolan Galway didn't believe women belonged in the U.S. Marines, but then a dangerous mission brought him and former marine pilot Rhona McGregor together. Though he'd intended to ignore his beautiful copilot, Nolan soon found himself wanting to surrender to the primitive hunger she stirred in him....

#1460 THE SECRET BABY BOND—Cindy Gerard
Dynasties: The Connellys
Tara Connelly Paige was stunned when the husband she had thought dead suddenly reappeared. Michael Paige was still devastatingly handsome, and she was shaken by her desire for him—body and soul. He claimed he wanted to be a real husband to her and a father to the son he hadn't known he had. But could Tara learn to trust him again?

#1461 THE SHERIFF & THE AMNESIAC—Ryanne Corey
As soon as he'd seen her, Sheriff Tyler Cook had known Jenny Kyle was the soul mate he'd searched for all his life. Her fiery beauty enchanted him, and when an accident left her with amnesia, he brought her to his home. They soon succumbed to the attraction smoldering between them, but Tyler wondered what would happen once Jenny's memory returned....

#1462 PLAIN JANE MacALLISTER—Joan Elliott Pickart
The Baby Bet: The MacAllister Family
A trip home turned Mark Maxwell's life upside down, for he learned that Emily MacAllister, the woman he'd always loved, had secretly borne him a son. Hurt and angry, Mark nonetheless vowed to build a relationship with his son. But his efforts brought him closer to Emily, and his passionate yearning for her grew. Could they make peace and have their happily-ever-after?

#1463 EXPECTING BRAND'S BABY—Emilie Rose
Because of an inheritance clause, Toni Swenson had to have a baby. She had a one-night stand with drop-dead-gorgeous cowboy Brand Lander, who followed her home once he realized she might be carrying his child. When Brand proposed a marriage of convenience, Toni accepted. And though their marriage was supposed to be in-name-only, Brand's soul-stirring kisses soon had Toni wanting the *real* thing....

#1464 THE TYCOON'S LADY—Katherine Garbera
The Bridal Bid
When lovely Angelica Leone fell into his lap at a bachelorette auction, wealthy businessman Paul Sterling decided she would make the perfect corporate girlfriend. They settled on a business arrangement of three dates. But Angelica turned to flame in Paul's arms, and he found himself in danger—of losing his heart!

SDCNM0802